GRAVEYARDS, VISIONS,
and other
THINGS THAT BYTE

Library and Archives Canada
Doidge, Meghan Ciana, 1973 —
Graveyards, Visions, and Other Things that Byte/
Meghan Ciana Doidge — PAPERBACK

Cover design by: Elizabeth Mackey

ISBN 978-1-927850-82-4

— *Dowser 8.5* —

GRAVEYARDS, VISIONS, *and other* THINGS THAT BYTE

Meghan Ciana Doidge

Published by Old Man in the CrossWalk Productions
Salt Spring Island, BC, Canada

www.madebymeghan.ca

Author's Note:

Graveyards, Visions, and Other Things that Byte consists of three novellas narrated by Mory, Rochelle, and Jasmine, and is set in the Dowser series. It is intended to be read between Dowser 8 and Dowser 9.

The Dowser series is set in the same universe as the Oracle and the Reconstructionist series. While it is not necessary to read all three series, in order to avoid spoilers the ideal reading order of the Adept Universe is as follows:

Other books in the Dowser series to follow.

More information can be found at
www.madebymeghan.ca/novels

For Michael
Fate? Destiny? You.

The warriors have fallen. And those they previously protected must now band together to keep the invaders at bay.

Mory, a young necromancer; Rochelle, a pregnant oracle; and Jasmine, a fledgling vampire, will do whatever it takes, whatever the cost, to prevent the fated future from unfolding. Even if that means they must become warriors themselves.

Mony

*A*n oracle was strolling along the paved path that cut through the graveyard, heading toward me. Even in the waning gray light of late afternoon, and even without feeling her footfalls resonate with magic through the ground I'd claimed, her practically white, bluntly cut hair was a dead giveaway. A beacon of her otherness.

Rochelle Saintpaul.

The late-December afternoon was chilly enough that the oracle should have been wearing a knit hat. At a minimum. I gently tugged four intertwined, variously colored lengths of fingering-weight yarn from my bag, knitting a few more stitches of the marled slouch hat I was working on, even as I tried to remember if I had any dark-gray cashmere yarn in my meager stash. It was an easy guess that the oracle's favorite color was black, given her choice of clothing—currently an extra-large black hoodie over faded black jeans—as well as her intricate arm sleeve tattoos. But I hated knitting with black. It was too easy to make a mistake, and to miss the error for long enough that I'd then be forced to unravel the entire item.

The Mountain View Cemetery was huge, stretching over a hundred acres across ten city blocks north to south, and two residential blocks wide. I was perched practically in the very center of all that sprawl, situated on my favorite tombstone. Surrounded by over 92,000 gravesites and 145,000 interred remains. And knitting, eternally.

The magic I commanded while on the property afforded me a certain amount of protection from the notice of nosy visitors, but it would do nothing to mask the oracle's presence in the cemetery. Still, even if nonmagicals laid eyes on either of us, they'd most likely assume we were merely visiting the grave of a loved one.

Though the chances of an oracle being in the cemetery for any other reason than to chat with me were super slim. Even nonexistent. And I didn't believe in coincidence. Magic tied everything together—every action and reaction all looped together in endless knots, ranging from the simplest constructions to the most intricate lacework, from birth through death and beyond.

I knew. I was a necromancer. The 'beyond' part of that equation, of that design, was my dominion.

I had spent the previous afternoon and evening with Rochelle, avoiding the witchy chatter at Jade's bridal shower, eating sushi at the dowser's apartment, then dancing at Jade's bachelorette party. Our parting had been swift—with me whisked away accompanied by Drake and Kandy, and the oracle dragged off by her husband, Beau, and Jasmine. The dragging part wasn't an exaggeration. Trouble had already been brewing in Vancouver. And then the oracle's magic had been triggered by the appearance of a horde of invading elves.

I hadn't questioned being hauled back to Pearl Godfrey's house and sequestered behind the heavy-duty wards of the head of the witches Convocation. All right, fine. I hadn't questioned the decision adamantly. I knew Jade wouldn't have been able to focus on kicking elf ass with me tagging along. The dowser was careful with me. Too careful. Because I wasn't the teenager with only a dim grasp of her magic who'd gotten herself kidnapped—twice—under Jade's watch anymore.

Though just because I could speak to the dead, it didn't mean I could fight my way out of a paper bag. Not unless I had access to a corpse. And that hadn't been pertinent in the context of the elf situation.

And actually, my being able to command the dead wasn't a particularly well-honed skill. More of an experimental theory, really.

Late last night—or way too early in the morning, depending on how you looked at it—while I'd been snoozing on Pearl's couch, Jasmine had shown up with news of whatever had gone down between the dowser's crew and the elves. Contrary to the orders of her master, Kett, the golden-haired vampire had doubled back after getting the oracle out of danger and on her way home. But that was all the information I could glean before the witches—including Pearl, Scarlett, and Olive, who was in town for the dowser's wedding—sequestered themselves away in the map room with Jasmine for forty-five minutes. Even Drake, who was a fledgling guardian dragon, hadn't been able to hear anything through the sealed door.

Then Drake and I had been sent packing. According to Pearl, a junior necromancer wasn't in any immediate danger from the elves. Plus, the big guns—aka Jade and her badass posse—were no doubt dealing with the situation.

I hadn't heard anything from anyone since. But that wasn't terribly unusual. Not only did Adepts usually prefer to keep company with their own kind, the warrior types that called Vancouver home often took off for days or even months at a time without notice. Then, out of the blue, Jade would show up back at the bakery to shovel cupcakes down my throat. So I wasn't particularly surprised that all the tension and the bodily forcing of necromancers and oracles into escape vehicles hadn't resulted in the end of the world.

I had no doubt that Jade could handle herself against the elves. I mean, backed by her fiancé, Warner, plus a werewolf and an ancient vampire, she was practically invincible. And an actual guardian dragon, Haoxin, had been in the mix as well.

I was also totally accustomed to how information filtered its way through the ranking Adepts. Vancouver was witch territory, with Pearl Godfrey overseeing everyone. And though necromancers were technically part of the coven, we were on the bottom of its roster of importance. Jade threw that balance out of whack, though, and I picked up a lot that I probably wasn't supposed to know through her. And from hanging out at the bakery during my weekly meetings with Pearl.

So even Jasmine being tight-lipped when she'd commandeered Kett's SUV and driven Drake to the bakery and me home wasn't at all unusual. Not that I was particularly chatty either, but Drake was. Usually. The previous night, though, the fledgling guardian had been seriously peeved about being kept out of the information loop. I'd actually never seen him as agitated as he had been before he'd gone home via the portal in the bakery basement.

As Rochelle spotted me, she stepped off the cemetery's paved path. It hadn't rained since the previous night, but the trimmed grass between the mixture of upright and flush-mounted headstones was still damp. All of Vancouver was almost perpetually damp from late October through April.

At the party, the oracle hadn't mentioned any pressing need to talk to me. So … maybe there was more going on with Jade and the elves than Pearl Godfrey wanted anyone to know? A cold wash of fear deadened my hands. I dropped a stitch, inwardly cursing but ignoring it for the moment.

"Is it Jade?" I practically shouted.

Rochelle didn't answer me, instead continuing to stride across the wet grass with her hands stuffed deeply into the pockets of her hoodie. She wore her faded black jeans long enough to drag at the back of her sneakers, and the bottom two inches of her cuffs were getting soaked.

All right, fine. All Adepts, even me, were well versed in the close-mouthed-about-magic-or-magical-happenings game. I shoved the rest of my questions—*Has something happened? Is everyone okay? What the hell is going on?*—back down and swallowed them. I forced myself to fix the mistake in my knitting before it unraveled through to the slouch hat's ribbed brim.

It was always better to appear outwardly calm around Adepts of power, anyway. And though Rochelle was only three years older than me, there was no question that she was powerful. I might not have been able to feel her type of magic when she wasn't within the cemetery grounds, but I had seen her oracle power streaming from her eyes the night before.

I finished knitting the row, slipped the skull-shaped marker that denoted the beginning of a new round, then continued. The moonstone stitch marker had been a gift from Pearl Godfrey for my nineteenth birthday last February, along with three skeins of cashmere from Sweet Fiber Yarns, and a set of interchangeable wooden knitting needles. Pearl, the chair of the witches Convocation, had taught me how to knit while she was pretending to mentor me. But in reality, I spent an afternoon every week at the bakery in the company of witches, a dowser, a werewolf, and even the occasional dragon, because every one of them was concerned about me going dark.

The possibility of my soul having been corrupted when I'd been kidnapped, tortured, and almost sacrificed—twice—by a black witch put them all on edge.

Because a black witch was destructive but containable. A dark necromancer was an entirely different issue.

So I went to my weekly meetings, and I tied myself and my magic to the cemetery. I kept my undead turtle, Ed, with me at all times as a focus, as an almost subconscious active strand of my power. Clearly I wasn't feeling evil yet. And the knitting helped, mostly because it helped me concentrate on wielding my magic precisely. But also because I liked making things. Being productive.

Feeling calmer, I glanced up. Rochelle had paused a few steps away. She was staring fixedly over the top of the headstones to the south.

I followed her gaze. A tall, medium-brown-skinned figure was prowling around the far chain-link fence that edged West Forty-First Avenue. The magic he left in his wake simmered at the very edge of my range, which ended abruptly at the boundary to the cemetery. I couldn't actually see his face from this distance, but there wasn't a terribly large black population in Vancouver. Which was a pity really, because Rochelle's shapeshifter husband Beau was really something to look at. With his green-blue eyes and chiseled features, he could have modeled for a living instead of working with cars. Even the three months of gray skies and rain we were suffering in Vancouver did nothing to sallow his complexion.

The same couldn't be said for me.

"You haven't heard anything more, then?" Rochelle asked, still watching Beau patrolling the perimeter. "Since last night?"

I wondered if the werecat was always this highly protective of his oracle wife—or whether it was the events of the previous night that had him on edge. "No. You?"

Rochelle shook her head. Then she pulled her phone out of an army-green satchel painted with boughs of ivy that were reminiscent of the sleeve tattoo the oracle had on her right arm. Not that I could currently see any of her tats. She didn't have any on her hands or face, and every other section of her skin was currently swamped underneath the too-large hoodie that also covered her rounded belly. The oracle was something like six months pregnant.

Rochelle glanced at the phone, tapping on the screen a couple of times. Presumably checking that she hadn't missed any text messages.

"So Jade or Kandy hasn't texted you?" she asked.

"Not yet." I returned my attention to my knitting, moving from plain garter stitch into a patterned section—knit four stitches, purl four stitches, over and over, slip the marker, and continue for eight rows. "But it's not like we text every day. And Jade's wedding is on Thursday. So they'll be busy with that."

Rochelle nodded. "I just thought someone might text this morning."

"Because of your vision?"

"Yeah."

She didn't elaborate further. And it was rude to ask about something so personal as an Adept's magic. And…well, if Rochelle had seen something yesterday or earlier today that had caused her to seek me out, I honestly wasn't certain I wanted to know. At least, I didn't need it blurted out, especially if the oracle didn't seem inclined to do so.

The conversation lapsed between us. Again.

Rochelle glanced around for Beau, apparently finding him over my right shoulder. Though it was difficult to tell exactly where she was looking through the dark-tinted, white-framed sunglasses she wore.

And I didn't want to stare. Adepts didn't like being stared at, including me. But at the nightclub, when Rochelle had been gripped by a vision, her eyes had shone white. A blazing white light that was a physical manifestation of her power. I'd never seen magic like that before, though I'd heard that some witches—and Jade—saw magic as an array of colors.

Jade wasn't just a witch, though. And if Rochelle's presence in the graveyard wasn't tied to the events that had ended the dowser's bachelorette party prematurely—before I'd had a chance to ask Drake to dance, which was honestly too bad—I had no idea why the oracle had sought me out. I wasn't certain how she'd tracked me down at all, really, except for her ability to see the future.

I shivered, tightening the orange-and-red gradient cashmere scarf I already had cinched around my neck, then zipping up my sweater more tightly. The extra-large Cowichan-inspired sweater, with its skull-and-crossbones design, had been another birthday gift. From Kandy and Jade, knit locally but custom designed.

"I'd like you to find my mother, if you can."

"Um, okay. She's dead, then?" Stupid question really, since I was a necromancer. But it was always a good idea to be clear about these things. "Like, you know that for certain?"

"Yes." Rochelle touched something through her hoodie. The chain of a necklace, maybe?

I had my own necklace—a magical artifact, really—that had been created for my protection by the dowser herself. Ancient coins of various sizes and shapes hung from a thin gold chain that was woven through the thicker links of a white-gold chain. Jade added another coin and another layer of her magic to the artifact every few months, fortifying a piece of alchemy so powerful that there had been whispers behind my back about me being the one to wear it.

There weren't many secrets that could be kept from necromancers, because there weren't many secrets to be kept from ghosts. Plus, Benjamin Garrick was writing a chronicle, so he was pretty nosy about anything and everything magical. The younger vampire was still fairly new in town, but he didn't mind trading information to get his questions answered. His snob of a mentor, Kett, was a total jerk—and also most likely the person who'd been doing the whispering in the first place.

But then, I really couldn't blame him. Vampires didn't trust necromancers any more than we trusted them.

"So ..." Rochelle prompted. "Will you look for her? Her name was Jane Hawthorne, not Saintpaul. Though she would have been cremated as a Jane Doe by the ministry."

"Interred at Mountain View? But why would she be ... she died in Vancouver?" As far as I knew, Rochelle and Beau had just moved to the city themselves about a year and a half before.

Rochelle shifted uncomfortably, shoving her hands so deep into her pockets that the fabric strained under the pressure. "I was born here ... lived here, in Vancouver, for the first nineteen years of my life."

"Really?"

She nodded. "My mother was killed in a car accident the day I was born."

"What? Seriously?"

"Yes. And she didn't have any identification on her."

Rochelle stopped talking, letting me piece together and then extrapolate the rest of her background. Different last name…mother dying after—or even while—giving birth…so the oracle was an orphan?

I knew that just because she hadn't mentioned a father didn't mean he wasn't alive. Though if he was, wouldn't he have known her mother's name, so that she wouldn't have been buried as a Jane Doe?

I opened my mouth to confirm my thoughts, then shut it without voicing the questions. Rochelle's disclosure was unexpectedly unsettling. But also, the why and the how weren't any of my business.

All right, then. I focused on my knitting, thinking over all the correct things to say in this situation. All the warnings and whatevers that a necromancer was supposed to give when an Adept approached them with a request. Because this was my first commission. Banishing shades, talking to ghosts, easing transitions—this was what necromancers did. Even raising corpses when supremely necessary. Usually such things would be done as commissions, working at the direction of the witches Convocation. Though some necromancers freelanced as well.

But not me. I was still in training. Sort of. Really, I was just on hold until my mother deemed me ready. Even more so than with other types of magic, necromancy grew more potent with age.

I was only nineteen, two months away from turning twenty. But it wasn't just my youth that had me in limbo. It was the fact that I'd spent too much time with Sienna—aka Jade's sister, and a black witch—against my will. And even though that didn't matter in the grand scheme of things, and it was four years later now, everyone was still waiting around to see if I was going to flip the evil switch as well.

I knit another row, then looked up at Rochelle. The oracle was gazing off across the graveyard again. "You know, it wouldn't actually be your mother, right? Just a shade. Assuming I manage to find anything even vaguely corporeal at all, given the fact she was cremated."

"How is a shade different than a ghost?"

"A shade is like an echo, occasionally of the person's last moments. Say, if their death was traumatic in some way. They can also manifest as a death loop. You can ask questions of a shade, but you might not get an answer. You might not be able to get any response at all. You know how sometimes you'll be walking along and get a random, all-body cold shiver? You might have just walked through a stationary shade."

"Really?"

I shrugged, keeping my attention mostly on my knitting even though I could work a simple pattern by feel. "Some say so. Anyway, a ghost contains some of the essence of who a person was. It's a remnant of their spirit, or energy if you like that idea better. Ghosts often remain in this dimension by choice, like they have unfinished business or they're looking after a loved one. Like how my great-uncle, Walter, chose to stay with my mom when he died. She was only two years old at the time, and Uncle Walter was the only family she had left. Occasionally, ghosts can also wind up trapped in this dimension. They can often communicate, present an idealized image of themselves, and occasionally even interact with our world. Briefly. And usually because a necromancer has fed some of their own magic into them."

Rochelle was staring at me. Her normal, almost offish caution—which seemed to be her default when interacting with anyone other than Beau—had turned to outright wariness.

"Do you want me to continue explaining?"

"Yes, please."

"Some necromancers claim that there's a third level. That a person's spirit can be summoned, either for questioning or to briefly manifest. But the practice, if even possible, is … frowned upon. You know."

"Summoned from where?"

I gave Rochelle a look.

"You mean, like from heaven … or hell?"

"Everyone has their own belief system."

"But we're talking about magic, yes? And all magic has practical roots, fueled by energy, say from the earth itself."

"For witches."

"And necromancers?"

I shrugged again. "Did you know that necromancy really only passes through the female line?"

"I'd heard."

"Some people believe that's because only women can deal in life and death."

Rochelle snorted. "Plenty of people deal in death."

"But they don't harness it."

"So … you're saying that … death powers necromancers?"

"Sure. Makes sense, doesn't it? The energy released when someone or something dies triggers an ability in some people."

"And heaven and hell? Do you believe? I mean, if you summon my mother, you'll be pulling her from heaven?"

"No," I said, more sharply than I'd intended. "Summoning spirits is just conjecture. I don't … that's not actually possible. Not for me, certainly. And as for heaven…well, ghosts can't really talk about it. They can't discuss the different levels of existence."

"Like you ask and they can't answer?"

"Yeah. You ask and they blink out, or fade, or go all fuzzy when they try to answer. Like something is restricting them from talking. From transmitting."

Rochelle looked a little pale, a little shaken. But that wasn't unusual around necromancers. Even Jade with all her power got a little peaky when confronted by death magic.

"Something…as in God?"

"I can't answer that part."

"Are spirits…angels?"

"Not that I know of."

"Have you met an angel?"

"Nope. But I've met enough demons to tell you they aren't coming from hell. Just another dimension. Like the elves. Ask any of the dragons, they've been around the longest."

Rochelle shuffled uncomfortably. Though I wasn't sure if it was the mention of dragons or of demons that had put her off.

I opted to change the subject. "Why me? There are two more powerful necromancers in town. Why did Pearl Godfrey send you to me?"

"She didn't. I just see you here…in this graveyard."

I shrugged. "I come here often."

Rochelle hesitated.

I hated it when people hesitated before talking. It usually meant they were considering lying, or telling a half-truth. And then I was usually forced to go along with the lie like it was an actual conversation we were having.

"No. That's not what I mean." Rochelle shoved her left hand in her army-green satchel. Her tone was soft, as if she were afraid of frightening me.

Me. The necromancer fueled by death magic, who'd been freaking the oracle out only moments before.

"No. I see you." She tugged a thick fold of paper from her bag.

I knew what she was handing me even before she held it out.

A sketch.

Of me. Of my future.

I had never seen one of Rochelle's visions—the final version, rendered on paper—but people talked. All right, Jade Godfrey talked. Everyone else was pretty mum about anything having to do with power around me.

I took the proffered paper, feeling myself hesitating suddenly.

"It's not bad." Rochelle fiddled with a ring on her left hand. A gold wedding band crusted with tiny diamonds. Her husband Beau wore a matching one, though his was thicker. And according to the rumor mill, aka Benjamin Garrick, it adjusted in size whenever he transformed. Both rings had been crafted by Jade, the same as my necklace. "It just … is …" she said.

I unfolded the sketch. And there I was, rendered in black, smudged charcoal. I was perched on my favorite gravestone—the one I was presently seated on.

I had developed a habit when I was young, even before my necromancy had manifested. I had demanded to visit the graves and interment places of young children whenever I traveled with my mother while she was working—and would occasionally throw a tantrum if that demand wasn't indulged. I used to swear that the children would whisper secrets to me, though my mother always insisted that their essence had moved on.

That had been my version of imaginary friends. Though the gravestone I most identified with at Mountain View was different. The sweet soul interred beneath my feet occasionally made an appearance, and I...I was hoping that one day I'd have the ability to help her. To release her from whatever held her in this dimension.

"Your hair is different." Rochelle stepped up beside me and leaned closer, peering down at the sketch in my hands.

"Yeah," I mumbled, taking in every stroke and smudge on the paper. I looked...different. Different than I saw myself in the mirror. Fiercer, bolder. Just...more. I wondered if that was how Rochelle saw my magic, as if it added an extra layer to me as a person. "I change my hair a lot."

"No," Rochelle said. "It's different in the sketch...in the vision. Blue and purple, not the purple and red you have now. Were you planning on dyeing it again soon?"

I shook my head, unable to tear my gaze away from the drawing. "I just changed it from blue."

"Ah ..." Rochelle nodded thoughtfully.

"You, um...you see in color but sketch in black and white?"

She hesitated for long enough that I realized I'd overstepped, asking such a personal question. It was one thing to explain in general terms how something like necromancy worked, or to ask for specifics about the sketch I was holding. It was completely another thing to interrogate an Adept about their process. How their magic functioned, or even how it felt for them specifically. Magic was like sex that way. Not that I had much experience with either.

"Yes," the oracle finally said. "Things … I didn't know, you know, when the visions started, what was happening."

"You didn't have anyone to ask."

"No, I didn't. And when I was trying to make sense of it all, black and white felt more … grounded but less … real …" She trailed off, embarrassed.

"I understand. My mother works as a necromancer for the Convocation. And usually that means summoning ghosts to question them. Or, conversely, laying a ghost to rest who's getting all poltergeisty. But … three times now, she's had to go … examine, assess other necromancers. Adepts, but outside of any known bloodline, whose magic had manifested and made them think they were …"

"Crazy."

"Yeah."

Rochelle nodded, then looked back down at the sketch I was holding. "I get that."

I spent another moment contemplating the version of me depicted in the drawing. Then I asked the question I had to ask but really didn't want to. "So … there's no way this is just, you know, a casual thing? Right?"

"Me having a vision of you? Rather than any of the other epically powerful beings that come and go from Vancouver?"

"Yeah. That's what I thought." And that in a nutshell was why hanging out with people way more powerful than me was a bad idea. Except that everyone in Vancouver was more powerful than me, it seemed.

"So … my mother?"

I folded the sketch, carefully tucking it in with my knitting. "You still want me to look for her?"

"Yes. I understand you might not be able to speak to her, but I have this … feeling …" She didn't finish her thought.

"Like a vision? Your magic told you to seek her out?"

"No." Rochelle wrapped her hands over her belly. It was an unconscious gesture that called attention to her pregnancy, which she mostly hid underneath her cold-weather layers. "I've been thinking about asking you for some time. Since before we met, really. Since I first learned that necromancers existed."

"Do you know where her gravesite is?"

"No. I mean, not other than here. As I understand it, this is where the ministry inters unclaimed ashes. I figured out that much."

"Okay. I'll try to narrow down the location. She, um … your mom, Jane, died on the day you were born? From a car accident?"

"January 27, 1995. Saint Paul's Hospital, if that matters."

"Okay, there has to be some record of that. I'll start there and let you know how it progresses."

"Thank you. I, uh … I know that an offering is customary when asking another Adept to perform magic for you. Usually an exchange. But I didn't know if you'd want a reading from me."

I nodded, completely agreeing. "Can we bank it? I might not even find a trace of your mother, with her being cremated and all, so …"

"I can owe you. No worries."

I glanced over to where I'd last seen Beau, but he had stepped out of sight. "Interred remains are spread throughout the cemetery, but there are also a few walled columbaria where single urns are interred, as opposed to combined family units or in-ground spaces. We can start looking together right now, if you like."

"Sure, um…that would be good." Rochelle's shoulders relaxed.

I didn't know the oracle well enough to have picked up that she'd been tense before. And whether it was exposing her past or asking for a favor that had been bothering her, I still wasn't sure.

I tucked my knitting away—I hadn't yet figured out a way to walk and knit at the same time—and hopped down from the headstone. "You can ask Beau to join us, if you like."

"He's just, um …"

"Being overly protective?"

I was joking, but Rochelle leveled a look my way that wasn't amused at all. "Last night wasn't easy for any of us, Mory."

"I wasn't dissing Beau. Not exactly. Just…you can let him know that I'll know the instant anyone with magic steps into the cemetery, so he'll have a heads-up."

Rochelle frowned. "You can…you feel magic through the earth? Like a witch?"

"Nope. Not like a witch."

She glanced around disconcertedly. "So, um…the ghosts tell you?"

"Occasionally. But don't worry, there aren't any around right now. They aren't big on strangers. Or daylight."

"Okay …"

"I, uh…the cemetery is mine." I shrugged. "My territory. I can't feel anything beyond the fenced boundary, so I suppose an Adept could launch an attack from the sidewalk or street. But most magic wielding is a close-up affair, isn't it?"

"I guess someone could preset a spell."

"Like a trap?"

"Yeah."

"I'd feel that too. It would feel like ... like a smudge, I think."

Rochelle looked at me for a moment, and I just let her. It always seemed odd that necromancy unnerved other Adepts—except for vampires. That made perfect sense. Vampires usually just wanted to eradicate as many necromancers as possible, because we were capable of controlling any magic connected to death. The same power that made it possible for me to feel when someone wielding magic stepped into a cemetery allowed us to control dead things—corpses, bones, ghosts. And, if the necromancer was powerful enough, vampires. But I understood that process was a little iffy, resulting in many necromancers being slaughtered by bloodsuckers, because vampires were only mostly dead.

Or that was how they felt to me, at least. A combination of death magic, which of course called to me, and a deep thrumming spark that felt as though it fueled them. A dark, throbbing energy ... like a heartbeat, but without the actual beating, living organ.

With a really powerful vampire—like Kett, Benjamin's mentor, Jade's friend, and the executioner of the vampire Conclave—that dark energy was loud, tumultuous, almost overwhelming. And definitely, in my opinion, untamable. The necklace I wore made being around him a bit more bearable, but if Kett wanted to kill me, even on the grounds of a cemetery I'd claimed as my own, he could do it. All I would feel was a great wave of chaos coming for me. Then nothing.

Even though necromancy might be thought unnatural by other Adepts—witches, sorcerers, shapeshifters, and even the oracle standing before me—it was vampires that felt the most discordant to me. Mostly. With one glaring exception. Though I'd met only three vampires so far: Benjamin, Kett, and Jasmine.

"Okay," Rochelle finally said, tugging her phone out of her bag again. "We can stay for a bit. But then I think we'll go see if Jade is around and pick up some cupcakes."

"The bakery's closed today." I crossed the wet grass, heading toward the nearest columbarium—a wall of niches designated for cremated remains.

Rochelle followed, still texting. "Oh. Right."

"I was planning to stop by tomorrow."

"And you'll text me if anything is up?"

"You, uh … you haven't seen anything more then? Had another vision? Or?"

Rochelle shook her head, but she didn't seem happy about it.

"That's a good thing, right? Not seeing anything should mean there isn't anything to see. Right?"

Beau appeared a few steps ahead of us. He had likely been summoned by Rochelle's text, but still, I flinched. I might have been able to feel him on the grounds, but he could still move too quickly for me to track unless I paid constant attention. And paying constant attention like that would be really exhausting.

"Necromancer." The shapeshifter nodded a greeting.

I kept my gaze somewhere around the level of his chest. Not that I was worried about staring at him, but so I didn't need to crank my neck. He was over a foot taller than me. "Beau."

"So, we're ghost hunting?" Beau grinned at Rochelle, displaying very white teeth.

Honestly, I could almost feel some of his adoration splash against my left shoulder. "Something like that,"

I mumbled. "I thought I could do a quick scan and see what impressions I get. If we can find any dates that line up in this section."

Beau nodded, reaching over and linking his fingers through Rochelle's. "Sometime in 1995. Not necessarily January, though, because they might not have buried her right away."

"Right. Let's take a look."

The cloudy sky was darkening as I led Rochelle and Beau across the cemetery, but it was heralding the sun setting rather than rain. We made our way over to the white stone walls of the columbarium. While the oracle and shifter wandered nearby, quietly chatting and looking at headstones, I visually scanned the first two sections of niches designed to hold cremated remains, checking names and dates. Most of the stone panels affixed to the front of the niches were inscribed, though a couple near the bottom were blank. None were marked *Jane Doe*, *Jane Hawthorne*, or *January 27, 1995*, though.

I hunkered down at each of the unmarked niches, allowing a single strand of my necromancy power to uncoil from my fingertips. Reading human remains for gender and age at death was a fairly junior skill when it came to learning necromancy. Usually an early acquired ability. Instinctual, even. And most necromancers quickly learned to actively ignore that mostly passive, automatic side effect of their magic. Picking up specific characteristics—say hair color, eye color, and height—was a more refined skill.

I eliminated the first niche simply by checking if the unmarked remains had belonged to someone of the magical persuasion. They hadn't. Very few Adepts were buried in Mountain View—and those who had been were mostly witches, which made sense with Vancouver being coven territory. As far as I'd been able to figure out, all of those Adepts had chosen to be cremated. Because it made sense that people who knew necromancy existed would want to limit how much of their person could be called back to the earthly plane.

I couldn't get an immediate impression from the second unmarked niche, so I sent out a second and third strand of my magic, seeking any minute residual, any glimmer. But I got nothing. That was odd.

I brushed my fingers across the neighboring niche, immediately picking up that it held the remains of a tall, dark-haired woman with brown eyes who'd died at the age of fifty-seven. A quick glance at the inscribed name and the dates confirmed my impression. The niches above and on the other side of the unmarked compartment also easily yielded impressions.

"Have you found something?" Rochelle asked, quietly anxious.

I shook my head. "I don't think so. A blank. It's probably just empty."

I straightened, preparing to tackle the third walled row, when Rochelle started shivering. Beau wrapped his arm around her. And though neither of them was complaining, I suddenly felt stupid for dragging them around with me.

"Listen, I have your number," I said, pulling my phone out of my bag to confirm. "I can't see in the dark or anything, and I have something I have to do for the witches tonight, anyway. So let me try to figure out where your mother's remains might be, like more specifically than just wandering around, and I'll come back tomorrow."

Rochelle glanced up at Beau. He offered her a slight smile but no guidance. If that was what she wanted.

"Okay. You'll text."

"If I find her." I brushed my hand against the interment niches to my right, immediately picking up faint impressions of the remains held within. "No point in dragging you out here again if I can't."

Rochelle nodded, but I could tell she was disappointed.

"If we positively identify where your mother was interred and I can't get an impression, then I can always ask my mother to try."

"Thank you," Rochelle said. "And you'll text when you hear anything from Jade or Kandy? I usually drop off eggs at the bakery Tuesday afternoons, but my hens aren't laying consistently right now, so I wasn't planning on bringing any this week."

"I'll text either way."

"Can we give you a ride somewhere?" Beau asked politely.

"Thanks, but I'll find a car share." I gestured with my phone. "It's not a bad time of day to grab one around here."

Rochelle abruptly wrapped her fingers around my raised wrist. Her touch was icy, but I suppressed the need to flinch. Showing anything that could be interpreted as fear around powerful Adepts was a bad idea. Whether or not they intended you harm, it made you appear to be prey. And that kicked in instincts. It would likely be protective instincts in Beau and Rochelle, thankfully, but those could still feel suffocating.

Occasionally, though, acting like prey got you kidnapped by a black witch. Then dragged around Europe for months while she slaughtered Adepts and stole their magic.

The oracle didn't speak. She just held me lightly, for long enough that her skin began to warm against mine.

"Rochelle?" Beau asked gently.

She nodded, releasing my hand. "Something has happened," she whispered. "Something happened last night. I'm sure of it. But I…I can't see what it means or where it leads. I look, but I see…nothing." She glanced up at Beau. "Maybe seeing nothing is what death looks like for an oracle."

Beau touched her upturned face, running his fingers along her cheekbone and jaw. It was a gesture so full of…adoration…love…tenderness…that I had to look away.

"You had a massive vision last night," Beau murmured. "Different than anything you've experienced before. You're tired. You could easily be burned out."

Rochelle nodded. Then, turning to me, she smiled tightly. "Thank you for your time and efforts, necromancer."

"I will not fail you, oracle," I said—and in all seriousness. A trace of weight settled briefly on my shoulders, almost like the touch of a ghost. Then it ebbed away. It was magic, maybe, but not compatible with my own. Or perhaps my necklace had absorbed whatever energy had passed between Rochelle and me automatically. Repelling magic was what Jade had designed it to do, after all. That and stopping the ghost of my brother from stealing my life force.

But that was another story, another lifetime. For Rusty, at least.

"I know you won't." Rochelle's smile softened, becoming more sincere. Then she wrapped her arm through Beau's and allowed him to lead her away, keeping carefully to the paved pathway.

The oracle did look tired. Drained, even. But I didn't want to believe that her inability to clearly see whatever was going on with Jade and the elves—or whatever had gone on after we'd left the club—meant that she was peering into the abyss of her own death. Put simply, too many people would stand in the way of whatever might come for Rochelle. I doubted whether anything could get past Beau or Pearl for a start. And even if it did, it most certainly wouldn't get past Jade.

Thinking about Jade made me slip my hand inside my sweater collar, weaving my fingers through the scarf so I could curl them around my necklace. My friend Burgundy was a witch, and even though she couldn't see the necklace's energy, she could feel its power. She told me that both the chain and the coins Jade had connected to it with her alchemy teemed with magic.

I certainly didn't worship the dowser. I didn't put her up on any pedestal, didn't think she was infallible. But still ... I trusted her to always be there when she was needed.

I just kind of wished she didn't think I needed her quite so often.

I watched Rochelle and Beau walk away, crossing toward West Forty-First Avenue where they had presumably parked. Then I closed my eyes and sent my senses reaching out through the cemetery, careful not to disturb anything that slumbered in its depths. I tracked the magic of the oracle and the werecat, losing the feel of it—the aliveness of it—the moment they passed through the fenced boundary.

Their being alive was foreign to this place. It was what made any Adept who stepped onto land that had been claimed for the dead stand out. Except for vampires. If Kett or Jasmine had ever crossed through the cemetery, I hadn't been on the grounds at the time.

But when Benjamin Garrick walked through Mountain View, he felt like he belonged. Just as I felt like I belonged.

I wove my way back through the rows of the pale stone columbarium, pausing to touch the one that had felt empty to me. Without the worry of boring Rochelle and Beau, I took the time to really listen for the whispers it should have contained. Again, I easily picked up glimmers from either side, but I could sense nothing from within. It crossed my mind that maybe some family member had insisted on keeping the remains, even though the interment niche had been purchased and the name marker had been adhered.

But that would have been odd. Wouldn't it?

I brushed my fingers across the letters etched in the stone panel by my shoulder.

… daughter, beloved …

It was getting dark enough that I couldn't quite read the smaller lettering. I could have used the flashlight on my phone, but I just shook my head instead. I had more important things to do than stand around as the chill of the evening set in, manifesting mysteries where none existed.

I walked toward the main road, checking the car2go app for a nearby vehicle. The only reason I had the money to pay the credit card attached to the car service was because of the task I had to do just after sunset every night. Bus service wasn't the most reliable means of transportation in Vancouver, and Pearl Godfrey hated waiting around whenever I was late for our weekly appointments.

Pearl had capitalized on the opportunity to put me on the Convocation's payroll after the elves had broken out of the guardian prison hidden in the shoreline of Kits Beach. Though honestly, I enjoyed zooming around in the Smart cars that I could rent by the minute, and not freezing my ass off waiting for buses. So I had cheerfully accepted the task, and the stipend that came with it.

I parked the car in a permit-only spot on Arbutus Street, which was one of the perks of using the car-sharing service. Then I walked through the grassy park that stretched toward the Maritime Museum. A glance toward the Talbots' house—a newly painted, four-level Craftsman—confirmed that at least Tony had returned from Whistler. The basement windows of his high-tech sorcerer lair glowed with the light of his multiple computer monitors.

That basement was my second stop, after my first errand had been run. I could have just texted my request to Tony—helping me track down Jane Hawthorne's place of interment—but it was proper to ask for magically inclined favors face-to-face. Not that the tech sorcerer himself cared about Adept protocol. I, however, did. Another side effect of hanging out with those who were more powerful than me.

When it came to using magic of any kind, ignorance wasn't a defense. Certain boundaries were not to be crossed, so it was best that those boundaries were always clearly defined. Because when an Adept ignored those clearly marked lines, they could too easily forfeit all their other rights—including life and liberty. If Sienna hadn't killed him, Rusty would have been sentenced to death for the murders he'd participated in. The pack would have demanded his life. And the witches would have granted it.

I jogged down the steps to a section of Kits Beach that had been designated as an off-leash dog park.

Benjamin Garrick was already perched on a surf-and-sun-bleached log by the time I reached the sandy lower path. Though it was almost fully dark, a couple of people were still on the beach, tossing sticks into the rolling surf for a terrier and what looked like a shepherd cross. The water had to be freezing, but the canines didn't appear to mind as they gleefully crashed through the low waves to retrieve their prizes.

Benjamin was always on time, though he didn't appear to wear a watch and routinely misplaced his phone. I had a feeling that his reliability had something to do with the way vampires felt when the sun set. But I couldn't go so far as to suggest that the sun dipping below the horizon woke him, or anything like that. I had never outright asked Benjamin if he was dead during the day, as some vampire myths claimed.

One entire section of my mother's library was devoted to vampire lore. But it was mostly garbage generated to perpetuate the already-ingrained fear and loathing that existed between necromancers and vampires. As much of it as I'd bothered to read, at least.

Benjamin glanced up from his notebook as I meandered across the sand toward him. Then he looked back down to finish writing whatever he was currently working on. Pale skinned with an olive undertone, he appeared to be around my age, almost twenty. And he was. He just wouldn't age another day ever again—unless, of course, that was just another myth. I hadn't known Benjamin when he was human. He'd been living with his mother, Teresa Garrick, in Vancouver for almost as long as he'd been a vampire, about fourteen months. But Benjamin had only been allowed to wander as he willed for the last three months or so.

Teresa also happened to be a necromancer of some power, and my mother's new best friend. The Garrick family had once been known as rogue vampire hunters. But that reputation had been snuffed out when the family had all been slaughtered by vampires over twenty years ago. All but one. Teresa.

And now there was a vampire in the Garrick line.

Benjamin closed his black leather notebook, tucking it in his inner jacket pocket. He was wearing distressed black jeans with a dark sweater underneath a leather bomber jacket—a jacket I'd found for him at the thrift store the last time I went looking for cashmere sweaters. If I found any that weren't felted, I unraveled them, reclaiming the yarn, which I then overdyed with Kool-Aid and reknit.

Benjamin had to constantly be reminded that it was cold in Vancouver this time of year—at least to everyone else. Hence, my giving him the jacket. I had sewn in the inner pocket for his notebook and pen, though he also carried a satchel with him everywhere.

He waited until I was about two steps away to speak. "Kandy hasn't returned my texts from last night."

"Did something happen last night? I mean, with you?"

Benjamin pondered my awkward question. I was hesitant to mention that a bunch of us had been out partying when the elves had shown up, in order to spare his feelings. Which was stupid. He didn't care about cupcakes or dancing.

"Nothing specific," he said. "I just always send a report of the evening, and Kandy replies with a K. Or at least an emoticon. Usually a pile of poo."

Watching the dog owners at the shoreline as they attempted to lure their pets out of the water, I cast my voice low. "Something happened with the elves last night."

"A fight?"

I shrugged. "Not sure. Jade banished Drake and me back to Pearl's, and sent Rochelle, Jasmine, and Beau away as well before anything really happened. Other than a bunch of elves crashing Jade's bachelorette party. Pearl's acting like everything is under control, but Rochelle is…restless. And now you haven't heard from Kandy."

Benjamin's notebook practically appeared in his hand. I knew he must have reached for it and pulled it out of his pocket, but he sometimes moved so quickly that I couldn't track it. It was unconsciously done, I thought. He didn't have Kett's strength or mobility. Not yet, at least.

"Drake?" Benjamin asked. His pen was poised over a blank page.

"Sometimes I feel like I'm just a walking encyclopedia to you," I said. And a blush instantly flamed across my face as the inappropriate complaint tumbled out of my mouth. It was inappropriate because wanting to be perceived as more than just a source of information to Benjamin wasn't applicable…or relevant to our relationship as it was currently established—for numerous reasons.

The most important of those reasons was the fact that this was a working relationship. We had been commissioned by Kandy, who oversaw and enforced things like security in Vancouver, to keep watch on the elves' former prison. But unbeknownst to Benjamin, I was also supposed to be keeping an eye on him. To help ease him into a life among the Adepts that called Vancouver home.

So the chronicle and his questions were perfectly in context, perfectly appropriate. And indicating in any way that I wanted things to be different or deeper between us was just…stupid. Moronic.

Again, for many, many reasons.

Benjamin eyed me questioningly, then started to close his notebook.

I sighed, feigning an exacerbated tone to cover my own embarrassment. "Drake. No last name that I know of. Fledgling guardian—"

"A dragon?"

I nodded.

Benjamin started taking notes. His handwriting was cramped but readable.

"He's a friend of Jade's … and of Warner's, I suppose. Trains with them, I think."

"Weapons? Affiliations? You called him a fledgling?"

"Actually, I'm not sure who his birth parents are, but he's the far seer's apprentice. I've seen him wield a long, wide, golden sword."

"A broadsword? When?"

"In London. When Jade, Kandy, Kett, and Drake rescued me from Sienna. Drake tried to hack through the magically sealed sorcerer pentagram I was being held in. With his sword. Unsuccessfully."

Benjamin's hand stilled. Then he looked up at me, locking me in place with his dark eyes. As if I were suddenly the center of his universe. A smile slowly spread across his face, and suddenly he was … more. Just …

I couldn't explain it. He was just more.

"Are you going to finally tell me the tale of the black witch, Mory?"

My heart began beating wildly in my chest. I would have sworn I could feel my blood thrumming in the veins of my throat. I listed toward Benjamin, feeling him calling to me.

He frowned.

I tore my gaze away, looking resolutely out at the dark, churning sea.

Benjamin had no idea he could ensnare me so easily. Without even trying. Another blush flushed my cheeks.

"No," I finally said. I wasn't interested in discussing being kidnapped by Sienna. I wasn't interested in being seen as less than capable. I was me now, not me then. I was the person I wanted him to know.

Again, that was stupid. But it was also the truth.

Benjamin nodded, returning his attention to his notebook. "And ... Jasmine?"

Jasmine?

Oh, God. Why didn't he know who Jasmine was?

Benjamin glanced up at me, then down at his notebook. The tip of his fountain pen was poised over a blank page he'd titled *Jasmine*. "Is she a secret?"

"No." I hesitated. "I don't think so. I mean, Jade, everyone, thinks it's okay for you to be writing the chronicle, right?"

Benjamin twisted his lips wryly. "The notebooks are stored in Jade's bakery safe after I fill them. So I have to ask permission to retrieve one if I need it. And I'm still collecting information, transcribing interviews, so I haven't actually written anything so far—"

"Jasmine is Kett's ... child."

Benjamin gave me a quizzical look. "Why does that upset you?"

"Because ... because you didn't know who she is."

"I barely know Kett. And as best as I can guess, tracking mentions of him through the chronicles I've read, he's over a thousand years old. What are the chances he doesn't have any children?"

I cleared my throat, then forced myself to speak. "She's new. Like you. Even newer."

"New?" he echoed. "Newly remade? Did you know her before?"

I shook my head.

"But she's living here now...in Vancouver. And newly turned."

"Yes."

Benjamin wasn't writing anything down. I'd never seen him not at least jot down a few notes once he had a blank page ready and had asked his questions.

"Did my...mother make her a bracelet too?"

I looked away, trying to organize my muddled thoughts and disjointed feelings. The dog owners were drying their wet pets off with large colorful towels. I imagined sand getting everywhere when they climbed into their cars. Or maybe they were walking home to one of the apartment buildings situated along the seawall—

"Mory?"

"No," I said, still not looking at him.

Benjamin wore a bone bracelet on his left wrist, embedded into his skin. I'd caught a glimpse of it only once or twice, but I could feel it continually. Its seething magic—a necromancy working—kept him in control. In his mother's control. Its darkly tinted, churning energy almost completely engulfed the bright pulse of Benjamin's magic, keeping him confined. Stifled. Able to sit on the beach near humans, chatting with me without desperately needing to drain every last drop of blood from my veins.

"She walks among you all," Benjamin murmured. "Jasmine. Because it's Kett's ancient blood that remade her, that animates her."

He didn't sound upset. But he still hadn't written anything in his notebook.

"I thought you'd met. I think they've been in town for a couple of months."

Benjamin nodded, capping his fountain pen and closing the book.

I'd expected more questions, about Drake and Jasmine, and about what had happened the previous night. But Benjamin just kept his hand on his notebook balanced on his jean-clad knee, with his head bowed thoughtfully.

I wanted to know what he was thinking. And, utterly absurdly, I wanted to fix whatever had broken.

Then I realized he was so still because he wasn't breathing.

I turned away, glancing around at the now-empty beach. It wasn't like Benjamin needed to breathe, but doing so made him seem more human. Necromancers and vampires were ancient enemies, but Benjamin and I scoffed at the obvious prejudices of our elders—and blithely ignored that the fundamental differences between us were fixed. Unchangeable. Vampires were the walking embodiment of death magic. And that power was the dominion of the necromancers.

I had no need or desire to control Benjamin—quite the opposite, in fact. But that personal declaration came a lot easier when he was acting human. With Kett, or even with Jasmine and the little I knew of her, the boundary was very clear between us. I knew, deep in my soul, that the magic that fueled the executioner of the Conclave would be my own death if I ever tried to harness it. Because Kett was too powerful to be contained by a single necromancer.

I couldn't imagine how Teresa Garrick felt every time she looked at Benjamin. How she felt about controlling her own son, even if she could completely justify the bone cuff she'd embedded in his wrist. Without it,

Benjamin would have been locked away somewhere, possibly even chained, for years. Maybe decades.

I pulled my dead turtle out of my satchel as I crossed toward the cliff at the edge of the shoreline, just below the upper grassy park. The tide was low enough that Ed wouldn't get too wet during his trek, but I usually needed to let him dry a bit before I stuffed him back in my bag.

Benjamin didn't follow me. But then, he usually didn't. Not after the first time I'd introduced him to Ed, and we had watched the turtle walk through the witches' wards that hid the entrance to the elves' prison. Ed could cross through the magic only because of the charm I clipped around his neck. And, possibly, because he was dead. The wards weren't necessarily set up to repel him. But magic could be unreliable, and that wasn't something I cared to test.

When Kandy had asked me if scouting with Ed was possible, I'd requested the charm. I didn't make him wear the magically imbued dime all the time, though, because he wouldn't be able to pull his neck into his shell. Technically, the red-eared slider was a corpse, powered and kept from decomposing only by my magic. But I didn't really like to think of Ed that way, or to risk his safety.

Every evening after sunset, I used Ed to patrol the halls of the prison. He couldn't step into the three cells themselves, because the white-tiled rooms somehow negated magic, and I would lose him within. If I concentrated, I could see through Ed's eyes, but it was a weird feeling and an odd perspective, since he was a six-inch-long semiaquatic reptile. Plus, his eyesight wasn't great. So I checked only the key positions that I'd sorted out with Kandy, using a map she'd drawn me.

Mostly, I used Ed like a dowsing rod, feeling through him for anything out of the ordinary. I couldn't feel for magical traces the same way a witch or sorcerer could. But especially if I was using my own power, I could at least feel it if something had been altered.

Honestly, at the time Kandy had first suggested it, I'd felt like scouting with Ed was a make-work project. Yet another thing to keep me busy, focused, and using my magic benignly. Like the knitting. But after the previous night—after the elves confronted Jade in the dance club, and those of us with fewer sword-wielding, elf-slaughtering capabilities had been bundled off to safety—I'd come to the realization that Kandy was just trying to keep a check on every little possibility. Anything, no matter how remote, that might tip the balance. The elves were an unknown adversary—and quite possibly many moves ahead of us in whatever deadly game was being played.

I glanced back at Benjamin. Using Ed had been his mother's idea. Or, more specifically, Kandy had gotten the idea of using the red-eared slider to scout after talking to Teresa at Jade's engagement party. Teresa had an affinity for birds. Dead birds. I'd overheard her talking about trying to acquire a raven from an aviary over on Vancouver Island, after it had passed on naturally. My mother preferred to work with ghosts—her uncle specifically, who she had kept tied to her since he'd died when she was a child. But even still, she had a bone collection that occupied almost as many shelves in our house's library as the books did.

I set Ed down in the sand about two feet from the rocky cliff. Any closer and the witch magic anchored in the stone would attempt to convince me that I needed to go home. I stroked his hard-shelled back. He blinked, then shimmied into the sand like he was contentedly scratching his belly, though I wasn't sure he felt such things anymore. I checked that the tiny witch charm was secured around his neck. Then I fed him a little more of my magic, giving him a mental push.

Ed crawled forward, moving steadily through the sand.

I stepped over to a nearby log, sat down, and pulled out my knitting. The yarn running from my work in progress to the wound balls nestled in my bag mimicked what my connection to Ed felt like. As if a long tether of my necromancy was unwinding as the turtle slipped unhindered through the witches' wards, then paused so I could take a look through his eyes.

I closed my own eyes, which made it easier to focus. Visualizing the tether between Ed and me, I mentally traversed the energy that bound us until I could see smooth rock underneath me and a sheer, smooth wall to either side.

Sensing nothing off or unusual in the mouth of the tunnel, I sent Ed onward, pulling my attention back to my hands and to the steady clicking of my knitting needles as I churned through stitches.

Benjamin had settled on the surf-bleached log to my left.

I could feel the low, slumbering pulse of his magic. And, before I could quell the impulse, I was imagining what that energy would feel like if it were freed and connected to me. Tethered like the yarn steadily slipping through my fingers. Knotted, woven together with my own magic until we were—

No.

That wasn't how it would be between us.

And it was foolish to romanticize a possible relationship anyway. Love wasn't about binding another person to you against their will. And Benjamin could never love anyone who had the capacity to control him. Who could? Plus, necromancy lore dictated that vampires weren't even capable of love, just lust. And that was only for blood.

But whether or not he was a vampire, Benjamin was also a person. He wasn't Ed. He wasn't the corpse of my pet, or a ghost to be used and moved as I willed.

I opened my eyes.

"Everything okay?" Benjamin asked.

He meant everything with Ed. Because that was our job. To check that the elves hadn't returned, to watch that no one else messed with the prison, and to report back. There was nothing more between us, and there never could be.

"Yes."

After carefully brushing dried sand from Ed's webbed feet, I ran my fingers over his carapace, checking him for any soft spots or other signs of decay. Perpetually fueled by my magic, whether I was wielding it consciously or not, Ed might well have remained in an undead, re-animated state for dozens of years. But magic wasn't always predictable. And if decay ever set in, spreading because I wasn't paying attention, I might not have the power to reverse its effects.

Benjamin abruptly closed his notebook. He slipped back into the shadow of the cliff face.

I glanced around, seeing nothing but a dark stretch of sandy beach and hearing nothing but the surf behind me. Then a dark-haired sorcerer stepped into the pool of light at the top of the concrete steps that ran down beside the Maritime Museum from the grassy park. He scanned the shoreline, spotted me, and jogged swiftly down the stairs.

Liam L.T. Talbot. A newly promoted Vancouver Police Department detective in his midtwenties. Brother of Tony, Peggy, Gabby, and Bitsy. He was currently dressed casually in jeans and an unbuttoned wool jacket, with a machine-knit scarf knotted loosely at his neck. But everything about him was a little too starched for my personal taste.

Or at least that was what I told myself. Because otherwise, I'd be forced to admit I just didn't like sorcerers in general. And that prejudice was based in fact and experience, not just an ingrained reaction to anyone who was remotely different than me.

A sorcerer had teamed up with Sienna. Two different sorcerers, actually, though only one of them was still alive, as far as I knew. In Oregon, Blackwell had run from the greater demon that he'd help summon, leaving the cleanup to Jade, Kett, and Desmond. And in London, Sayers had turned against two of his own and had tried to kill me as part of a ritual demon summoning.

So, surprise—I didn't trust sorcerers as a rule. And no one blamed me. Not even Jade, who liked to like everyone.

Though Liam's brother Tony was different. His kind of sorcery dealt in tech, not the accumulation of magical objects. Or demons, for that matter. Tony hadn't ever given my necklace a second glance.

The same couldn't be said for his older brother. Or either of his parents, for that matter.

If I hadn't been inclined to dislike Liam, I might have thought him handsome. His skin was naturally tanned, and he was fit enough that even the loose T-shirt he was wearing underneath his open jacket stretched across his chest. His dark eyes were shot through with green and blue, and he had strong, capable hands.

Not that I'd looked at him all that closely.

Not much, anyway.

"I thought I'd find you here." Liam strode across the sand between us like he owned the beach. His accent was clearly American, but my ear wasn't good enough to narrow it down by state. "I thought that bloodsucker was supposed to be watching over you."

"He is," I said mildly, carefully brushing sand from Ed's hard-shelled underbelly.

Liam stuffed his hands in his front pockets and rocked on his feet, like he would have preferred to keep moving but was being forced to stop and talk to me. "Anything to report?"

I gave him a withering look.

He was gazing at the cliff face, maybe feeling the magic of the witches' wards or sensing Benjamin in the shadows. As such, he missed my effort, forcing me to be disparaging out loud.

"No," I said. "Not that you're the one to ask."

"Yeah... while things get sorted, I'll be taking Kandy's rounds for a bit, checking on you in the evenings and Burgundy in the mornings."

Burgundy, my friend who was training in witch magic with Pearl and Scarlett, was tasked with checking on the thirteen points of the witches' magical grid every morning. It was a task that took her all around Vancouver, from the bridges that crossed to the North Shore to the boundaries of Burnaby and Richmond.

"And why would that be?"

"I'm just helpful like that," he said, smiling.

"What things need to be sorted?" I asked, fishing to see if he actually had any insight into what was up with Jade and Kandy. If anything was up at all. "And on whose authority?"

He shrugged. His smile lingered, but there didn't seem to be anything behind it. "I volunteered."

I stared at him.

He glanced away.

Right. If Liam was going to be a closemouthed asshole, I'd just go on with my personal plans. I tucked Ed into my bag, intending to brush by the sorcerer, planning to treat him as inconsequentially as he was treating me. Then I decided to take him down a notch at the same time.

"You know I was with them last night," I said, turning back to address him.

"What?" Liam feigned confusion.

"With the elves. At the dance club."

He frowned. I could actually see him reassessing the situation and all the assumptions he'd made about me—and specifically, about my relationship with Jade. Yeah, I was close enough to the dowser that I'd been invited to her bachelorette party. Close enough to whatever was going on that he really should have just fessed up whatever he was so obviously hiding.

Mory 1, sorcerer 0.

I started toward the stairs, glancing over to where Benjamin was standing in the shadows, watching our exchange. I could feel his magic even though I couldn't see the vampire. Liam apparently couldn't even do that.

"See ya, Benjamin."

Liam, following a couple of steps behind me, stumbled.

Mory 2, sorcerer 0.

"I have my phone." Benjamin's disembodied voice filtered across the sand.

I nodded, reached the base of the stairs, and started climbing.

Liam paused, looking back toward the cliff again.

I stifled my sneer, rather pleased to leave the stuck-up sorcerer in my wake.

Unfortunately, he caught up to me just as I was crossing the seawall path into the grassy stretch between the beach and the houses on the edge of Kits Point. I was still intent on asking Tony to help find Jane Hawthorne's interment site for me. Unfortunately, the Talbot at my heels wouldn't have any problem following me into his family home while I made the request. And I wasn't interested in getting interrogated about things that weren't any of his business.

"I didn't mean to suggest that you didn't know what was going on," Liam said, matching my stride. That wasn't a difficult task, since he was easily ten inches taller than me.

I didn't bother answering.

Liam wasn't daunted by my silence. "So that turtle of yours... it can walk through wards?"

I glanced over at him. "Why?"

He shrugged. "Just an idea I'm formulating."

"When you decide to let us peons in on your plans, then I'll answer your questions."

"Hey, I'm not sure what I've done to piss you off, but ..."

I waited for him to finish his sentence. He didn't. I assumed that meant I was supposed to offer up an explanation for myself. I laughed snarkily.

"Only you can figure out your own prejudice, sorcerer."

Liam stayed silent.

I paused at the curb, giving him a moment to decide if he wanted to share while I glanced both ways for traffic along Ogden. But Liam didn't pick up the conversation, so I crossed toward the Talbot residence without another word. The thought crossed my mind that I probably should have texted Tony to tell him I was dropping in, but he never left the basement voluntarily. And Liam had distracted me.

"Maybe I'm still figuring out how everything works here," Liam said quietly, walking behind me again.

I glanced back at him. "Really? Defaulting to being nice until being antagonistic becomes necessary? You find that confusing?"

He clenched his jaw. "There are a lot of different definitions of being nice. I protect—"

"Please. We all look after each other. We don't demand it as a right. Plus, you're really only interested in protecting those you don't deem beneath you."

"How do you get that?"

I laughed snidely. "Um...how about calling Benjamin a bloodsucker? That's shortsighted...especially for a sorcerer."

"And how does the magic I wield make any difference?"

I shook my head with a sneer. Then I made my way to the sidewalk on the other side of the wide street and crossed the Talbots' front lawn. The basement windows were still the only ones lit. Liam watched me go, stuffing his hands in his pockets again.

I glanced back as I cut along the path between the side of the house and the fence. The sorcerer's expression was grim. Thoughtful, but stressed.

Necromancers weren't the only Adepts who hated vampires. But in Vancouver, everyone was welcome. Including the Talbots. Jade and Kandy made it so.

Tony Talbot had transformed the basement recreational room of his family's home into a technological haven. When I'd first been invited to a games night by Peggy, who was a telepath, I'd assumed that all the Talbots lived under one roof. But I hadn't also realized that four of them were sorcerers, including Tony and his parents. The twins, Peggy and Gabby, along with their elder sister, Bitsy, were adopted. Liam, who had moved to Vancouver a couple of months earlier than the rest of the family to start his probationary period with the Vancouver Police Department, had rented an apartment somewhere in the city and had kept it. Certainly, if I was a twenty-three-year-old sorcerer with an apartment all to myself, I wouldn't have given it up for a room over the garage either.

All right, yeah. I knew way too much about someone I didn't even like.

The back door was never locked when someone was home—and hadn't been since Jade kicked it in three months earlier. Regular door locks couldn't bar the magically inclined from entering, and especially not anyone of Jade's power level. Plus, replacing a door was a hassle, even with Kandy having arranged for a maintenance crew to fix it straight away. Pearl Godfrey was the Talbots' landlord, after all.

I had to cross through the laundry room, bypass the stairs into the kitchen, wave at a camera set in the open-stud wall, and execute a secret knock on the door to gain entry. The knock was a bit of a joke between the rest of us, and something Tony had insisted upon implementing after Jade had trashed the place. The dowser had blown through like she usually did, rescuing all of us after Gabby's magic went wonky and amplified all our powers past the point of control.

Afterward, the tech sorcerer had declared that he wouldn't have been quite so hasty in throwing magic around if he'd known who was coming through the door. The fact that the dowser had been standing in the room for at least a minute before Tony stupidly attacked her—and got easily trounced for the effort—didn't seem to dissuade him from his argument. Neither did installing the camera that had arrived a few days later, along with numerous boxes containing a new TV and just about every product that Apple manufactured. Burgundy told me that it had been Kandy—not Jade, who really wasn't Tony's biggest fan—who had replaced far more than what had been destroyed in the so-called amplifier incident.

So yeah, Tony's version of events ran a little differently than what I'd experienced.

I executed the secret knock a second time, then stepped back to wave to the camera. Because the main problem with Tony's security measures? He usually wore headphones while working, and his parents wouldn't actually let him install a lock on the door because it was supposed to be recreational space for the entire family.

"Come!" Tony shouted from within the room.

I entered into the harsh light of his monitors, immediately flicking the switch to my right to turn on the overhead lights.

"Hey!" Tony howled, covering his eyes.

I ignored him. I had no problem sucking up to Tony with the secret knock, but I wasn't going to try to have a conversation with a sorcerer in the dark. Though honestly, that had less to do with his magic—he was different from any other sorcerer I'd ever met—and everything to do with the fact that he was a nineteen-year-old male who never left the basement if he could help it.

Tony squinted at me. He was dark-haired and tall, with light-brown skin like his brother, but the resemblance ended there. Tony would need at least twenty pounds of muscle, a haircut, and a daily shower if he ever wanted to be as uniformly clean-cut as Liam.

Except for the shower, the same could be said for me. And even then, I'd never measure up in the looks department to someone like Jasmine, who was epically gorgeous, or even to Jade, who surpassed being simply pretty with the force of her personality. So why bother?

In that indifferent attitude, Tony and I were the same. Other than that, we were completely dissimilar. And not in an opposites-attract sort of way.

"Mory," Tony grunted, turning back to his main computer screen—a twenty-four inch monitor. He had two desks set up in the far corner of the room, with multiple monitors placed right against the walls. Every inch of both desktops was covered in electronics.

The first thing Tony had done upon receiving Kandy's gifts was to crack open the box of each and every laptop, iPad, phone, watch, and other tech device to fiddle with them. He had some process for making them his own, tying them to his specific brand of sorcerer magic. Even the huge TV, wall mounted so that it was centered in the room, now responded to his verbal commands. Though not always reliably.

The center of the large rec room was occupied by a huge sectional couch and a large square coffee table, which was currently strewn with controllers for at least three different gaming systems. Friday nights at the Talbots' house were reserved for board or card games. Anyone who wanted to play just had to show up by 9:00 P.M.

I'd been wanting to invite Benjamin for a while, but I hadn't yet. He'd met Burgundy and the twins, Peggy and Gabby, at the bakery. But I was worried about how Bitsy and Tony would react. Apparently, werewolves and vampires didn't mix. Like, on an instinctual level. And no matter how contained and calm Benjamin's bone bracelet made him, Bitsy was still in denial of her own second nature. She was reluctantly training with Kandy, but she still had trouble changing into her wolf form.

And Tony?

All right, fine. I was slightly concerned that Tony might be interested in me. Too many casual comments had been dropped by third parties—the twins and Kandy—about us hooking up to ignore. And, for some reason, I didn't think the sorcerer would take to Benjamin very well.

"You just going to stand there?" Tony asked. His fingers hadn't paused their frantic movements across his keyboard. Text scrolled up his screen, but I couldn't see what it was from my vantage point. "There's cola in the fridge." He made a halfhearted gesture toward the small black fridge to the far left of the desk.

"No, thanks." I wandered across the room, trying to figure out how to phrase my request without ending up owing Tony a favor. That was underhanded, sure. But I didn't want the payment to be some sort of an attempt at a date. "Just bumped into Liam."

Tony grunted but didn't otherwise respond. I could hear tinny music emanating out of his headphones, which he'd removed to leave slung around his neck.

"Have you ever met an oracle or seen a … prediction?" I asked, super casually pulling the folded sketch that Rochelle had given me out of my satchel.

Tony spun in his chair—and realized belatedly that he looked overeager. He leaned back to mask it but went too deep, almost toppling backward. Recovering his balance, he took a swig of pop. The can was empty.

Flustered, he set it down on the desk and folded his arms across his chest.

"You know an oracle?"

"Yep. Rochelle." I untangled a strand of yarn that was trapped in a fold of the sketch, but I didn't open it. "She draws. And she was the one who figured out how to make the map part of the witches' grid work."

Tony sneered affectedly—as sorcerers always seemed to do whenever witches were mentioned. But he was clearly struggling to hold himself back from snatching the sketch out of my hands.

I unfolded the sketch, pretending to study it. "I was in the graveyard today—"

"Mountain View?"

"Yes. And Rochelle stopped by and asked me to find someone for her."

"Someone dead?"

I gave him a look. "What else would anyone ask a necromancer?"

"Right, right. And?"

"When I asked her why she was asking me, she gave me this." I handed him the sketch.

He took it gingerly. Handling it only by the very edges, he shoved two keyboards and a disassembled phone out of the way to clear a spot on the desk, gently placing the sketch down. Though there was more than enough light in the room, he stood up and flicked on a desk lamp, repositioning it over the image.

He stared down at the vision of me rendered in charcoal.

Intently.

Then he found, cleaned, and put on a pair of thick glasses I'd never seen him wear before. He stared some more.

I pulled out my knitting, leaning back against the desk.

"What's the connection?" Tony finally asked, not looking up from the charcoal rendering of me perched on my favorite headstone. "From this vision to the request she made?"

I shrugged, knowing that the less I told him up front, the more interested he'd be in helping me out.

"Maybe it's the grave you're sitting over," he murmured. "Can you make out the name?"

I could, but only because I knew it.

"Maybe there's a mystery you need to solve. Like a murder? Or switched bodies? And you need to find the real victim?"

"She gave me a date of death and a name," I finally said, keeping my attention on my knitting as if I were just casually filling him in, not asking for information. "But the ashes would have been interred as a Jane Doe."

That got Tony's attention off the sketch. "At Mountain View?"

I shrugged. "Rumor has it."

A wide, cocky grin spread across the tech sorcerer's face. "Hit me with it."

"DOD January 27, 1995. Jane Hawthorne. Died at St. Paul's Hospital after a car accident as a Jane Doe."

Tony turned back to his computer, pulling his main keyboard slightly forward, then stretching his hands and wrists. "Child's play."

I reached for the sketch.

"I'd like to keep it." Tony said, rapidly opening browser windows. "In case there are any more clues."

"It's … mine," I said. I felt suddenly and oddly awkward about having shown it to him at all. "It's … I should keep it."

Tony nodded, picked up his phone, and snapped a picture of the sketch. It was all done perfectly casually. Then he glued his eyes to his monitor screen.

I folded the sketch and tucked it in my satchel. "I have some research to do myself. Necromancy stuff. Text me when you have anything?"

He nodded absentmindedly.

I slipped away. But when I turned back at the door, I saw that he had sent the picture he'd taken of the sketch—the picture of me—to his computer. And that it now occupied one half of his screen.

That was…oddly disconcerting. But I had presented it as a clue. I brushed away my reaction as I called back, "Thanks, Tony."

He waved his hand over his shoulder, acknowledging me. Though he could have just as easily been waving me away, as he might a fly.

And I had a much, much easier time with that assessment. I exited the Talbots' basement and headed home.

Mom and I lived in an older Georgian manor in Shaughnessy, which had way too many rooms for just the two of us. On occasion, the guest rooms got filled by visiting necromancers who wanted to study or consult with my mother. The door to Rusty's room hadn't been opened since he'd been murdered by Sienna, even though he had moved out a couple of years before his death into an apartment downtown.

The front door was unlocked, but the house was empty when I got home. I hadn't seen my mother for a couple of days, but that wasn't unusual. The Convocation kept her pretty busy. And she really didn't like being at home. Not since Rusty died.

I locked the door behind me, not bothering with lights as I wandered back across the huge main floor to the kitchen. I poured myself a bowl of cereal from a random box I grabbed off the shelf without looking, then took it with me into the library.

The house had been part of my father's inheritance, not from my mother's side of the family. His ancestors had come with the Godfreys to the Pacific Northwest to establish a coven. Of witches.

Necromancy was rare. Probably more so than any other magical lineage, because its traits usually fully manifested only in the female line. Apparently, it was a thing for female necromancers to marry the male offspring of other necromancy families, given the option. But my mother, whose entire family had been dead by the time she was two, had been raised by witches. Accordingly, she fell in love with and married a witch. My father.

My dad had died before I was born. But no matter how many times Rusty or I had asked, we never got the full story about what had happened. I knew it was something bad. Something magical. But my mother, who dealt in death magic daily, couldn't bring herself to talk about it. Not ever.

The one thing I did know was the fact that the Godfrey coven didn't contain a single other male witch, even to this day. That was a little more than odd. But I hadn't yet gotten up the courage to ask Pearl about my father. I had meetings with her where we did nothing but knit, so I'd had plenty of opportunity. But I knew there was a chance I wouldn't want the answer.

One of the bonuses of hanging out with the head of the witches Convocation at Jade's bakery—besides the free cupcakes—meant that a lot of conversations and other meetings took place around me while I appeared to be totally distracted by my knitting.

Liam Talbot would have been shaken to his elitist, prejudiced core if he knew even a third of the things I did about the business of the Godfrey coven. But then, I'd lived through a chunk of the Adept drama that had shaped the coven myself. If it could even be called a coven anymore.

I flicked on the lights in the library. Thousands of books lined the dark-stained oak shelves built into the walls, ranging from literary fiction to necromancy tomes. Supposedly, there was some sort of befuddlement spell on the magical texts, so that our house cleaner—who came twice a month—couldn't see them. But I couldn't feel it. It was witch magic, renewed yearly by whatever coven member was available.

My father's familial line—the branch that wielded witch magic—had died with him. I'd inherited my mother's necromancy, which was carried by both sexes but usually only manifested in females. Rusty had been a witch, though not much of one. He'd had a minor affinity for plants and could cast spells as part of a group of witches, but magic hadn't really been his thing.

Magic was like that. Two really powerful Adepts could, on occasion, have less than magically stellar children. I knew that Pearl thought magic was dying, like how the earth was dying. Which would make sense for witches, who pulled their power from the earth. But I wasn't sure the same would hold true for other Adepts.

I took my bowl of cereal to the far table, setting it down along with my satchel. Then I wandered over to the book-lined shelf nearest the window that looked out at the overgrown backyard. Necromancy texts were grouped together, most of them handed down through my mother's family, with the occasional new addition. Unfortunately, the mostly leather-bound books weren't organized, at least not by any means I could figure out. Plus, I didn't really know what I was looking for ... shade-summoning magic specific to interred remains, maybe?

The shelves to my far right were lined with the skeletons of various animals—my mother's bone collection. It was mostly skulls, but occasionally, she found perfectly preserved smaller animals like mice or birds.

I wasn't interested in collecting bones. I had Ed. From the time he'd been the size of a loonie, he'd lived in an aquarium in my bedroom. And when he'd passed away two years before, I had removed the water but kept the tank. When Ed wasn't in my bag, he hung out there, digging in the sand and rearranging small pieces of driftwood.

Finding nothing specific to cremation in the titles etched on the spines of the books on the highest shelf—at least the highest one I could reach without a stool—I selected the first three leather-bound volumes with the word *grave* or *graveyard* in the title. I had to start somewhere.

Turning back to the table, I grabbed a bite of my cereal. And I had just opened the first book when the skull of a rat seemingly levitated off the middle shelf to my far right. The skull slowly rotated, as if scanning the library, then settled on staring at me. A soft red glow emanated from its eye sockets.

"Hi, Freddie," I said, flipping a page of the book.

The rat skull swiftly but noiselessly dropped onto the shelf and went still. The shadow leech's energy—I could feel more than see it—ghosted past three mice skulls and a muskrat before settling into one of my mother's prize possessions. A beaver skull that still had its buck teeth, though one was badly chipped.

The shadow leech infused the beaver skull with its energy, once again floating it from the shelf. Then Freddie held that position, waiting for me to notice him…or her…or it. I wasn't certain the shadow leech—being composed of a mishmash of soul magic as far as I was aware—had a defining gender.

Either way, Freddie had first followed me home from the graveyard three months previously, and apparently loved playing with my mother's bone collection. Though I didn't think the leech had ever entered the house while she was home.

"Are you hungry?" I asked.

The beaver skull didn't dip or nod in response to my question. The shadow leech and I had never actually communicated, and I had no idea whether Freddie could speak. But I didn't have the guts to ask Jade, who had warned me off trying to tame the leech. So if Freddie did speak, it was on a level I couldn't hear.

"Teresa borrowed some of the bird bones on the top shelf this weekend. Maybe there's some residual on them?" I flipped another page. I didn't know whether Freddie was shy, or simply concerned that I was capable of hurting it. But either way, if I was too attentive, the leech would leave.

It was important that the shadow leech fed on magic that it was actually allowed to consume. I had a strong notion that it would only take one slip, one indiscretion, for Jade to decide that Freddie was too much of a liability. And since the demon part of what animated the soul mishmash couldn't be vanquished, that would mean death.

The beaver skull set itself down again. Then the shadow leech's energy slipped upward, eagerly flowing across the bird skeletons that decorated the top shelf.

Someone rapped on the window.

I jumped. Then I felt the pulse of magic behind me. Benjamin.

I turned back to see the dark-haired vampire peering in through the glass. He offered me a smile, then made a motion indicating that he wanted me to let him in.

"The front door would be easier," I said, casting my voice loudly enough to hopefully be heard outside the house.

Benjamin tapped again.

Shaking my head, I put the book down beside my cereal bowl and wandered over to open the upper window. The lower ones were fixed.

Benjamin rested his palms on the dark wood frame. Then he somehow lifted himself, slipped through the tight opening, and landed on the glossy hardwood floor beside me in a single smooth motion.

Right.

Vampire.

It was stupid how easily I could forget what he was.

Benjamin was already moving through the room, marveling at all the books as if he wasn't sure which one to read first.

I shut and locked the window, wandering back to settle at the table with my cereal. "Anything related to magic is shelved to my left and behind me."

Benjamin immediately corrected his course and began reading the spines—those that were titled, at least—without touching the books.

I opened the second of the three volumes I'd selected, flipping from the first to the final pages in the hope that it had an index or a table of contents. No such luck. I'd have to scan the entire text, looking for keywords. I sighed, opening my phone to make notes—and realizing as I did that I hadn't let Benjamin see Rochelle's sketch.

The vampire would likely be thrilled to see the oracle's magic rendered on paper. Enthralled, even—in the same manner as he was currently enchanted by the books in my mother's library. But I wasn't certain I wanted to share it with him. Somehow, the sketch hadn't meant as much to me when I'd leveraged it for Tony's tech help. That had felt like...business. But watching Benjamin while he examined the sketch...while he saw me as the oracle had rendered me...felt like it would be intimate. Beyond intimate.

But that feeling wouldn't go both ways. Benjamin would be gazing at magic. Not at me.

Ignoring the ridiculous bent of my thoughts, I started a new note, filling it with possible keywords: *cremation, summoning, unidentified remains ...*

"What are we looking for?" Benjamin asked, not taking his eyes from the shelves.

I stifled a smile. "I thought you couldn't see through witch magic."

That got his attention. "The books are spelled?"

"The magical ones."

A wide grin spread across his face. I quickly looked away so that I didn't get accidentally ensnared.

"So?" he prompted. "You're researching something."

I nodded. "Summoning spells that'll work specifically with cremated, unidentified remains."

"You need to talk to the ghost of someone who was cremated?"

"The most I can probably hope for is to access a shade. But yes, for Rochelle. The oracle. She asked me to find her mother."

Benjamin delicately pulled a book from the shelf. "Okay. Summoning spells for cremated remains."

I looked down at my bowl of cereal. "Yeah. I need something to help me narrow my focus. Pulling more than an impression from ashes is advanced necromancy. But I don't think you can help with selecting an actual spell. It, um... has to speak to me when I read it. It has to feel right."

"But I can help you make a list, at least." Benjamin smiled thoughtfully, settling down across from me while maintaining the same careful distance he always did. He opened the book he'd chosen and began to read. His hair fell across his brow and he unconsciously brushed it away. His fingers were long, almost delicate looking—

I tore my gaze away, finished my cereal, and focused on the book in front of me.

Hours of reading and five skimmed books later, I knew the exact moment my mother stepped into the house—because Benjamin was gone. I literally felt a breeze rather than saw him move. I was partway out of my chair, staring at the open window, when my mother barreled into the library. Her magic was tightly coiled around her—a dark, snakelike smudge ready to strike out.

Specifically, ready to strike out at the vampire she'd felt in her home.

I glowered in her direction.

The ghost of Uncle Walter hovered in the doorway, half hiding behind his niece, half egging her on. He darted his wild eyes around the room, twisting his hands together. My great-uncle had been attached to my mother ever since he'd died, vowing to never leave her side. And his sense of the macabre was warped, even for someone with only a latent ability in necromancy. As a ghost, he continually chose to present himself in the brown tweed suit he'd died in, still marked on his right shoulder by splattered blood from a head wound.

Uncle Walter also claimed to have been killed by a vampire while defending my mother in a cemetery. What he was doing in a cemetery with a two-year-old after dark, and why his murderer hadn't actually bitten and drained him, probably had more to do with the broken blood vessels that reddened his nose and his cheeks even in his 'idealized' ghost state. Yes, my mother's uncle was an alcoholic even as a ghost. And I had never seriously believed that a vampire had wandered into a graveyard on the estate of known necromancers, murdered Walter, and then left a baby necromancer behind.

My mother's step faltered as she cast her gaze around the library, settling on the pulled-out chair sitting opposite mine at the table.

I crossed over and closed the window.

"Ben," she spat. Her Croatian roots echoed in the name even though she'd never lived in Europe, somehow turning it into an insult.

"Yes." I settled back at the table, suddenly incredibly tired. "You didn't have to run him off."

"It's ridiculous that the witches have partnered you with him."

"You and Teresa are friends."

"Friends!" My mother's dark hair fell about her face with the renewal of her anger. Fine streaks of gray where her hair was parted caught in the light. Her eyes were shadowed. Hollow, like she hadn't slept for days. "Teresa is a necromancer. Vampires don't have friends."

I closed the book I'd been scanning, sliding it to the side and pulling a final unread tome toward me. I didn't bother fighting any further with my mother. My silence would piss her off more than my words would anyway. Sullen silence—paired with the relationships I was continuing to cement in Vancouver—reminded her that she was of the older generation. And if the elders of the coven didn't adapt, they were going to find themselves left behind.

My mother dropped her overnight bag in the wood-cased doorway, striding into the room to her bone collection. Once there, with her fingers slowly caressing mandibles and cranial ridges, her magic settled. Thankfully, Freddie had left over an hour ago. Benjamin had been completely unaware of the leech's presence. I didn't like pointing out magical things to the vampire that he couldn't sense on his own.

But my mother wielded more power by accident than I did with intention. She was also twenty-seven years older than me.

"What are you working on?" she asked without looking at me. "Something for Pearl?"

"No. Rochelle. The oracle."

My mother half turned to me then. Suddenly I was all interesting. "Based on a prediction?"

"She doesn't make predictions. She sketches visions of the future."

"Yes. I know."

I flipped the page of the book I was hunched over, really just pretending to read. My eyes ached.

My mother circled the table, casting her gaze over the books spread across it. "The oracle wishes to speak to the dead?"

"Her mother."

"Ah, I see." And with that piece of information weighed and rejected as nothing more than routine—and therefore boring—I was uninteresting once again.

My mother picked up my empty cereal bowl, managing to not launch into a lecture about eating in the library. She really must have been tired. Then she crossed back toward the doorway. Uncle Walter had disappeared, though that didn't necessarily mean he'd wandered off.

I half expected my mother to shut off the lights as she left.

She didn't.

But as she picked up her bag, I forced myself to swallow my pride and ask for her help. The summoning spells I'd found specifically for working with ashes appeared complicated, and none of them had 'spoken' to me so far. And to judge by the number of books with the word 'grave' in their titles, I had at least thirty more volumes to dig through. I was eager for a shortcut.

"Mom?"

"Yes?"

"I was scanning cremated remains today—"

"At Mountain View?"

The interruption was annoying, but also somewhat relevant. Since Mountain View Cemetery was my claimed territory, my magic should have held a good deal of influence on the grounds. "Yes, but—"

My mother waved her hand. The one not holding the cereal bowl. "Ashes are advanced work."

She started to turn away.

I stood, trying to temper my anger at being so quickly dismissed. "I had no problem pulling impressions from the interments. Most of them." Mentioning the blank spot I'd found would only make me look even more inadequate than usual, so I kept that anomaly to myself. "But once I figure out the location of the cremated remains, I'd like to try a summoning spell."

"Mory...the older the ashes, the more difficult it will be to connect. How long ago did the oracle's mother die?"

I clenched my fists. "In 1995."

My mother smiled, not unkindly but a little too smugly. "You're young, Mory. Other than the vampire, Pearl has you focused on the right tasks. By the time you are in your midthirties, you'll be able to name every corpse in a graveyard just by stepping through the boundary."

"And that's the point at which you'll actually pay attention to me, then? Actually teach me something?"

My mother stared at me, but I couldn't read her at all—other than her overriding and constant frustration. She turned away, speaking over her shoulder. "Yes. Then I'll teach you."

When I was ready. When I was worth the time investment. When I was worthy.

A kinder person would have pointed out that all the loss my mother had endured was the root cause of our relationship issues. She'd grown up without parents, guided through her own necromancy by Uncle Walter. She'd fallen in love with a witch, who had died before meeting their second child. Then she'd lost her eldest, who had already been something of a disappointment.

Though based on the preservation of Rusty's room upstairs, I might have been making assumptions on that last part. But my only other narrative option was that my mother had loved her son more than she loved me.

A kinder person would have been able to look past her mother's faults, embracing the relationship we had managed to forge, no matter how flawed. But whether or not it was an irredeemable fault, I just wasn't all that emotionally evolved. The distance she maintained—the void between us, reminding me of the empty interment niche I'd stumbled upon that afternoon—hurt.

I shut the book that I wasn't actually reading. Then I returned all the books to the shelves and headed upstairs to my bedroom.

Setting my alarm for 9:00 A.M. gave me four hours to sleep, and an hour to get to the bakery before it opened. I put Ed in his tank and climbed into bed.

I hauled myself out of bed with my alarm. Then I just stood in the middle of the room, trying to remember why I was up so early.

Bakery. Checking on Jade. Before opening. Right.

I tapped the screen of my phone, accidentally snoozing the alarm instead of turning it off. Seriously, why did the app keep switching up which button did what?

Grumbling, I quickly checked that I hadn't received an update text that would alleviate the responsibility of the task I'd set for myself, giving me permission to climb back into bed.

No such luck.

I cobbled together a passable outfit, then topped it with layers of hand knits, including my red chunky-knit poncho with the beaded fringe. I was awake enough to remember that the clacking while I walked totally irked Jade. Though amusingly, the dowser had begun to visibly force herself to not nitpick every little thing I did that bothered her.

I tucked Ed into my satchel, double-checking that I didn't get him tangled in that day's knitting. I had a stock of reclaimed, Kool-Aid-dyed cashmere yarn that I was in the process of turning into arm warmers.

Heading downstairs, I grabbed two new books from the library that appeared to contain summoning spells, stuffing both in my bag in case I didn't have time to come home before heading back to the cemetery. I was working with the assumption that Tony would have a location for Jane Hawthorne's interment soon. I ate another bowl of cereal—shredded wheat, this time—while finding and reserving a car share a couple of blocks away. Then I was out of the house, and without having run into my mother.

I dropped the car in a permit parking spot on Yew Street, and another member of the service was already climbing into it by the time I'd wandered the half block to the alley that ran behind West Fourth Avenue. Cake in a Cup, Jade's bakery, would still be closed, but I wasn't planning to go in via the front door.

Approaching the steel exterior alley door situated between industrial-sized garbage and recycling bins, I suddenly felt a bit out of place. I'd never before been a person who felt the need to check up on Jade. It was actually kind of the dowser's job to check up on all of us. But I had told Rochelle that I would do so if neither of us had heard from Jade or Kandy by morning.

I knocked on the door, feeling a slight resistance from the wards that coated the building as I did so. Then I stepped back. I didn't usually feel magic other than necromancy that way, but Jade was uniquely powerful. The knocking was more polite than necessary. The dowser would have known I was outside the moment I brushed the wards. Hell, she might have even sensed me walking up the alley.

Gabby Talbot opened the door, already frowning. "Mory?" The tall, slim amplifier had her long straight blond hair pulled back into a ponytail. A streak of cocoa powder was on her cheek.

"Hey, Gabby. You're baking today? Alone?" Tuesdays through Saturdays were usually Jade's baking shifts, but she was getting married that week. It would make sense that she'd asked Gabby to cover for her.

Gabby glanced around the alley behind me, then gestured for me to enter without answering.

I stepped into the kitchen with my stomach already grumbling at the sweet scents of baking. The sight of a multitude of colorful cupcakes occupying almost every flat surface only increased my appetite. There were full muffin tins by the large ovens waiting to be baked, and tins on the counters that were baked but not iced. A tall steel rack near the swing doors that led to the storefront was more than half filled with trays of cupcakes ready to be placed in the display cases and sold.

Gabby closed the door behind us, promptly crossing back to the stainless steel counter that took up the center of the kitchen. She was frosting a batch of chocolate cake bases with what appeared to be a chocolate buttercream. "Todd should be here any minute."

My stomach rumbled again. I ignored it. Jade would have offered me a stool and a cupcake. Gabby did neither. The amplifier wasn't terribly friendly, though she and I got along well enough. But no one was as friendly as Jade.

"So you're baking?" I repeated my question. "On a Tuesday?"

"Liam texted," Gabby said. "Told me I needed to open and bake … until further notice."

Until further notice? And since when was Liam running or scheduling or overseeing anything? "And Jade?"

"Not here."

"Kandy?"

Gabby shook her head, switching frosting bags and carefully piping what looked like plain buttercream icing onto the remaining chocolate bases.

"So ... no one has heard from them since Sunday night?"

Gabby shrugged, then she glanced my way. "Liam knows something, but he's not saying."

"Jade's gone away before. For months sometimes."

"Without warning? And with Kandy?"

I wasn't exactly sure how dialed in Gabby, or even the Talbots in general, were with who Jade truly was—and with everything that had happened since Sienna had gone dark. But our current conversation didn't feel like a great time for a history lesson that it wasn't my place to teach. "And Scarlett and Pearl haven't been in?"

"The bakery was closed Sunday and Monday."

Right. "Okay ..." I watched Gabby frost another cupcake, not really knowing what else to ask her. Then I wandered back toward the door while inwardly mourning that I was leaving without eating. I could have waited for the bakery to open, then bought a cupcake. But still.

"That's it? You were just checking on Jade?"

I paused with my hand on the doorknob. "Yeah. But I'll just text her. And Kandy."

"Oh. I thought you might want my help with something ..."

I didn't get whatever the amplifier was hinting at.

"Tony said he's looking into something for you?"

Okay, Tony had a big mouth.

I must have looked peeved, because Gabby raised her gloved hands. "No details or anything. My brother is as cagey as the rest of you. It's just, I thought ... it might have something to do with Jade being gone. Like an assignment. And if Peggy and I can help, we'd like to."

Suddenly I felt like an idiot for being secretive. "It's nothing like that. Just an unrelated request from Rochelle."

"The oracle?" Gabby asked, far too casually.

Honestly, I was surprised that Rochelle didn't keep herself locked away at all times. Every Adept thought they wanted their future read. But as far as I could judge by my own experience, it was better to not know what was coming. I just nodded in response.

And then I remembered what my mother had said about not being powerful enough to work with ashes yet.

Gabby was an amplifier.

"Hey, um…you might actually be able to help. What do you think about coming to the graveyard with me later today and giving my magic a tiny boost?"

Gabby laughed quietly—perhaps because she was remembering the last time she'd boosted my magic. That amplification hadn't been tiny at all. It had embedded so deeply within me, spilling my magic so far and so fast, that even I had started worrying about what dead things I might awaken. Thankfully, by the time Jade had finally intervened, I'd managed to pull only dead animals forth from the Talbots' yard—mostly rats, mice, a couple of bats, and a few dead pets. But what were the chances that no humans had ever been secretly buried in a neighborhood that was hundreds of years old? For all I knew, there might even have been an undiscovered First Nations burial site in the area. And I certainly didn't want to be involved in covering something up of that magnitude.

"Not every girl dreams of being invited to a graveyard to help a necromancer speak to the dead, but I do."

Gabby gave me a rare smile. Then she reached across and plucked a cupcake from a grouping on the far side of the counter. "*Solace in a Cup.* That's one of your favorites."

I nodded, stepping back to take the chocolate carrot cake with chocolate cream-cheese icing from her. "I like the cinnamon. Thank you."

It wasn't really the cinnamon that made these particular cupcakes stand out for me, though. It was the fact that Jade had developed the recipe, along with three others, when we'd both been in mourning. Me for Rusty, and her for Sienna. Even though everyone around us thought our siblings had gotten what they deserved.

We hadn't talked about it. Not out loud. But …

It was the first cupcake Jade had ever given to me.

A weird combination of emotions suddenly gripped me—fear, sadness, anger, trepidation. Jade hadn't just gone off hunting elves somewhere with no cellphone service. Jade was missing…or worse. Otherwise, Liam wouldn't have been stepping up to take charge. Otherwise, Jade's mother, Scarlett, or her grandmother, Pearl, would have been at the bakery…or Kandy…or Warner…or even Kett.

"You okay?" Gabby asked.

I shook my head. Then, realizing that was the wrong response, I nodded. I'd been gripping the cupcake too hard, leaving the impressions of my fingers in the paper-wrapped, moist cake. "I'm fine."

If Jade or the others were missing or dead, there wasn't anything a lowly necromancer could do about it. So I would stay focused on finding out where Rochelle's mom was interred, and trying to call forth her shade. And by the time I got that sorted, everything else I couldn't control would sort itself out. Whichever way it went.

"Text me." Gabby glanced up at the clock on the wall, then went back to frosting cupcakes.

"I will." Cradling my cupcake in my hand, I pushed open the door and stepped out into the alley.

As the door clicked shut behind me, I slipped my hand underneath my poncho and looped my fingers around my necklace. Then, with Jade's magic in one hand and a cupcake in the other, I lifted my face to the gray, cloud-filled sky. And even though if pressed, I wouldn't have been able to definitively tell you I believed in any higher power—I wished ... I prayed for Jade to be okay.

Then I ate the cupcake, texted Rochelle my lack of news as an update, sent a 'checking in' text to Jade and Kandy, and headed home to crawl back into bed.

An incoming text message forced me to admit I wasn't really sleeping anymore. I opened my eyes to find a dead red-eared slider watching me from the neighboring pillow.

"Ed," I muttered, my eyes and throat sandy. "That's creepy."

Though, honestly, it was me who'd brought him to bed in the first place.

As I rolled over to reach for my phone, I thought about all the times I'd heard that necromancers glowed to the dead and the undead—beckoning to them with our magic. I'd never had it personally confirmed, but that might have been what Ed saw when he looked at me. A glimmer of my power.

The text was from Tony. Not Jade or Kandy. I swallowed my disappointment, along with the renewal of the gnawing fear that had kept me restless and wakeful for the entire morning.

>*Liam has an idea. Meet us in the basement in an hour?*

I groaned, texting back.

I'm seriously not interested in coming all the way there for an idea of Liam's.

Tony texted back an LOL emoticon. Apparently he thought my disdain for his brother hilarious. Then he added:

>*And bring Ed?*

That woke me up, just a little. Why Tony or Liam might have been interested in Ed, I had no idea.

Fine. I'm not sleeping anyway.

>*That's my girl.*

I stared at his last text for a while. I definitely wasn't Tony's girl, but I didn't want to be a snippy asshole about it when I'd just asked for his help.

Groaning again, I flung myself out of bed for the second time that day. It was later than I'd thought—after one o'clock—so I had probably slept somewhat.

After I showered, I texted back.

On my way.

I deftly avoided the 'my girl' subject by giving Tony the text equivalent of a combination cold shoulder and subject change. Hopefully, he'd get the idea.

"You want to do what?" I asked, crossing my arms and cradling Ed protectively against my bulky Cowichan-inspired sweater.

Obviously taking my indignation as rhetorical, Liam didn't bother repeating his initial request. "Do you think it could work or not?" The dark-haired sorcerer paced the length of the sectional couch that stood between us, only half addressing me.

I didn't like how rattled the cool and cocky detective had become in only a few hours.

"It will totally work." Tony was hunched over a tiny piece of tech on his desk. He appeared to be trying to figure out how to attach a thick elastic band to it.

"Magic and tech do not work well together," I said. Emphatically.

Liam glanced over at me, then gestured dramatically toward Tony. The tech sorcerer.

Ed, picking up on my rising anger, tucked his head underneath my thumb. I gritted my teeth, trying to remain civil. "Let me be clearer. My magic, necromancy, doesn't work well with tech. Plus—"

"Have you tested it?" Tony asked without looking up from his fiddling.

I ignored the interruption. "Plus, the witches' charm allows Ed to pass through witch magic, not elf magic. I'm not going to risk him—"

Liam laughed snarkily. "He's a dead turtle, Mory."

I almost turned and walked away. Topped by his already supremely false sense of self, the sorcerer's arrogance was completely ignorant. "What's this really about, Liam? You want to be a hero? Why don't you leave that to the actual warriors?"

He snorted. "Your so-called warriors have fallen, Mory."

"So you say."

"So I saw."

"They get back up. I know, I've seen them do it. Multiple times."

"Not this time. Jade—"

I was around the couch and in Liam's face before he could finish his sentence. He stumbled back a step as if I'd pushed him.

"Jade is bigger and badder than you could ever hope to be, sorcerer." I layered every ounce of contempt I could into that last word. Which, even by my estimate, was a lot.

"That's exactly—"

"And she's also the most decent and warmhearted person you will ever meet."

"I know."

"You don't. You can't even fathom it. You're arrogant and power hungry and completely ignorant of how magic actually works."

"Hey, now—"

I shoved Ed in Liam's face. He took another step back, coming up hard against the coffee table and almost tumbling backward. Tony was watching our exchange with his mouth hanging open.

"How do you think necromancy works, asshole? You think I just channel a piece of magic from the earth, or a magical artifact like you do, and funnel it into a corpse and voila!?"

"Of course not."

"So what do I use, then?"

"You … you use your … internal magic."

I laughed harshly. "To read graves or talk to ghosts, yes. But Ed isn't either of those things, is he? He's undead. He can even make certain basic decisions for himself. Say, if he senses danger or wants to explore his surroundings. What do you think fuels that, sorcerer?"

"I … I …"

"He's mine. A piece of me, asshole. Some necromancers work with bones and even blood to summon and bind."

"And the others?" Liam asked calmly. "What do necromancers like you use?"

I looked away from him, choking back the story on the tip of my tongue. A story about finding my brother's ghost. About giving him the strength to attack his murderer, Sienna. The story of how my own brother would have drained me, killed me, in order to avenge his death—and with so many people saying that he had been just as complicit in murdering a half-dozen werewolves as Sienna was.

I reached up, unzipping my sweater slightly so I could touch my necklace. Cradling Ed in one hand, I ran my thumb across the ridges on the lowest coin. It was an ancient inscription I couldn't read, on a piece of alchemy that had saved my life multiple times. Including stopping Rusty and Sienna from taking more than I had to give.

I calmed myself. "Soul magic," I murmured. "That's what I do. That's how I wield. Instinctively. Ed is animated with soul magic. My life force."

Tony snapped his mouth shut with an audible click of his teeth.

"And that rather brilliant magical artifact around your neck?" Liam asked gently. "Jade's work?"

"Yes." I met his gaze. "Try to take it off me, sorcerer, and you'll get a nasty surprise."

He frowned. "I think you've mistaken me for someone else."

I laughed darkly. "You haven't proven to be one bit different."

Liam's expression became stony. But then he nodded, turning back to look at Tony. "You're going to need something sturdier than an elastic. And we'll test the connection on witch and sorcerer wards before trying to breach the elves' ."

I shook my head, tucking Ed into my satchel. "You haven't heard one thing I've said."

Liam scrubbed his hand through his short hair, making it stand up in multiple adorable directions. I looked away.

"I heard everything. And I'm countering it all with the simple fact that Jade is in trouble. She needs our help. She'd do the same for any of us, yes?"

"You can't even comprehend what she would go through to rescue any one of us."

Liam smiled tightly. "There's your answer. If we do everything to protect Ed but still lose him to the elves, lose the sliver of your soul along with him ... and manage to save Jade in the process?"

I clutched my satchel tightly, feeling Ed shift within its depths. "The witches—"

"The witches are fooling around with their stupid grid," Liam said. He started pacing again, but slower this time. As if moving and thinking were the same function for him. "Trying to contain the problem. Wait it out. Avoid confrontation, not solve it."

"And your plan solves it how?"

"It gets us eyes on the elves and whatever the hell they're doing. Maybe it tells us why they need Jade. How they're ... holding her. Knowing that will help us figure out what to do next, before this spills out into the streets and threatens the entire city."

"You really saw them ... the elves ... carrying everyone into BC Place? Kandy, Kett, Warner, and Haoxin? Like, unconscious?"

"Or dead."

Fear tightened in my belly. "Except for Jade."

"She was carrying the blond woman."

"Maybe it was a ploy."

"Which is why I waited." Liam glanced at his wrist, tugging back his sweater to look at his watch. I didn't know anyone else who wore a watch these days. "Which is why I went to the witches first."

"The dragons—"

Liam scoffed. "When the city is in ruins, the dragons will bestir themselves. If they bother to come at all. Honestly, I'd thought they were a myth before meeting Jade—"

"Don't be an idiot. Haoxin is a guardian."

"Exactly. And this is her territory, yes?"

I nodded curtly.

"So if she's already here, then the other guardians will leave it to her, won't they? If I understand it correctly, they all oversee different territories."

I felt a little lightheaded. "Jade … Jade is the warrior's daughter. He'll come for her."

"They haven't come, Mory. Maybe they have reasons for that, but that's not my immediate concern. Because what if it wasn't a ploy? What if everyone is still alive? And what if they're killed because we waited?"

I swallowed hard. I willed myself to ignore my fear of failing, my fear that the task was too difficult, too far above my power level. Gathering every ounce of bravado I could muster—every ounce I had somehow collected through some sort of spiritual osmosis from those more powerful than me, to whom such things came naturally—I nodded. "But not without Jasmine."

"Jasmine? The vampire?"

Ah, there was that arrogant tone the sorcerer wielded so well.

"Jasmine," I said condescendingly, "was a highly skilled tech witch before she was remade. She's been working on the witches' grid, but if we can tear her away and she gives your plan her blessing, then yes. Yes, to save Jade I'd sacrifice more than Ed. I owe her, three times over."

"You want me to…consult a vampire?"

"You want me to hunker down with only you and Tony as backup—?"

"Actually, I'd be monitoring the feed from here," Tony interjected. "But Jade did mention that I should ask the vampire for help with my research into the elves."

I waved him off. "You want me to help you get through a massive magical shielding that the elves have erected over BC Place, sitting out in the open and practically blind as I pilot Ed. You think they won't notice?"

"That would be the idea."

"That's what you're hoping, Liam. Hoping. So yeah, I'll take the uberstrong, uberfast, tech-savvy vampire over you any day."

Tension ran through Liam's jaw. Then he shrugged his shoulders. "She'll have to come here. And I didn't want to delay until after sunset."

"No problem," I said, pulling my phone out of my bag. "She walks during the day."

Surprise flittered over Liam's face.

I smirked at him. "Let me give you a little piece of advice, sorcerer. You ain't in Kansas anymore."

The dark-featured sorcerer smiled wryly. "Boston. But, yeah, I get your point. Shut up and listen."

I nodded. "And stay out of the way when the swords come out."

"Right. Though it's possible you're also underestimating me, necromancer."

"Doubt it. But I'm not going to make you prove it. If what you're saying about Jade and the others isn't some ploy, and they've all fallen … then … we're probably all screwed."

Applying my thumbs to my phone, I crossed over and sat down on the couch while texting Jasmine. I was going to have to figure out how to word the request concisely, with just enough information to get the tech vampire to join us.

"Hey, Tony," I asked. "You got a location for me yet? For Jane Hawthorne?"

"I've got a general area for you to look, but I haven't been able to drill down further. The records might be offline." The word 'offline' was delivered with epic layers of disgust.

"Cool. A general location might be enough."

"I'll keep looking."

I had fallen asleep on the couch while studying a summoning spell that I'd found in one of the books I'd grabbed from the library. When I woke, I was clutching Ed, and the book was wedged underneath my left shoulder. I'd been pulled from my slumber by a pulsing, enticing energy.

Jasmine had arrived.

Though I didn't remember actually texting her the address.

I glanced at the coffee table, noting my phone a few inches from my face. I made a guess that someone—likely Liam—had continued the text conversation with Jasmine. So much for thumbprint security. Though I wouldn't have put it past Tony to have cracked my password.

I sat up, blurry-eyed and grumpy as all hell. I hated sleeping at random times during the day—though the darkened windows informed me that the sun was setting, and the day was gone.

"Not like that," Jasmine muttered, reaching over to fiddle with some tech Tony was working on at his desk.

The messy-haired sorcerer flinched, then froze.

Jasmine sighed as if completely put out. "Really? Get over yourself, child."

"Hey!"

"Well, do you want to do it right or not?"

"I'm not a witch. I can't just do it like you say just because you say it."

"Don't I know it."

Tony grumbled something under his breath. Then he bent back over whatever the two of them were working on together.

Jasmine turned her gaze on me. Her golden curls cascaded halfway down her back, and her bright-blue eyes were full of mocking mirth. "You introduce me to the best people, necromancer."

"Yeah," I muttered, stretching my legs over the coffee table. "Just wait until later." Liam had apparently left the room, if not the house.

Jasmine twisted her mouth wryly. "I've already met him. Delightful."

"Hey!" Tony said, though with a slight uncertainty that indicated he didn't quite know who we were talking about.

I settled Ed down in my lap as I remembered to take a picture with my phone of the summoning spell I'd been studying before falling asleep. Then I reached for my knitting.

The door opened behind me. A muted male voice preceded its owner from the hall. "I said stay out of it."

Jasmine's smile turned predatory.

"Screw you, Liam," Gabby said, shoving her way into the rec room with her twin Peggy at her heels. "We're already involved. Hey, Jasmine."

"Amplifier," Jasmine said, sounding slightly disappointed.

I read the vampire loud and clear. It was harder to mess with Liam when the twins were around. Gabby wasn't exactly friend material, but everyone liked Peggy. Plus, the twins were under Jade's protection. And no matter how powerful Jasmine was with the executioner's blood reanimating her, she wasn't any match for the dowser.

"Oh," Liam said snottily. "You're still here."

Jasmine laughed, sending chills up my spine. She had the same effect on Peggy, based on how the telepath rubbed her arms as she crossed through the room.

"Certainly you aren't suggesting you can't tell when a vampire is in your basement, sorcerer?" Jasmine purred. "That would be a rather exploitable blind spot."

"Nah," Gabby said, throwing herself down on the sectional couch next to me. "He's just pissed because you outrank him."

Liam sputtered behind us.

Peggy reached her hand toward Jasmine, offering to shake. The telepath liked touching people, using her magic. But not everyone was willing to take her up on it. "Hi, Jasmine."

The vampire gently grasped her hand. "Peggy. I see you all made it back from Whistler in one piece."

Peggy laughed. "We took a couple of falls on the hills but nothing serious. It was Gabby's and my first time snowboarding. But we've all skied before."

"And where are the rest of the Talbots this cloudy late afternoon?"

Jasmine's every word, her every interaction, was layered with the enticement that Benjamin exerted unintentionally when he got intrigued by something. The constant beguiling might have been unconsciously done on the vampire's part—or possibly even a sign of her relatively new magic simply leaking. But though the others didn't seem to notice, all I could hear was the vague threat underneath her luring tone.

Rationally, I knew that Jasmine would never hurt me. But irrationally, I occasionally had to force myself to stay in the same room as her. Being around her maker, Kett, was even worse.

"They'll be home in a couple of hours," Liam said. The threat laced through his tone was more than simply implied. So apparently, he sensed Jasmine's power, too.

"Bitsy had an indoor exhibition game this afternoon," Peggy said, still holding Jasmine's hand. "In the valley. For charity. Angelica and Stephan went with her."

"You'll ask them to consult with Pearl when they return?" Jasmine directed this question to Liam.

"Of course."

"All hands on deck would be appreciated."

"I'm the one who contacted you."

"No, sorcerer. Mory is the one who contacted me. You were prepared to drag the wielder's necromancer into danger without backup."

Tension ran through the detective's jaw. Again. He must have been a terrible poker player.

Peggy turned to look at me, still smiling sweetly. The light of her magic, as white as Rochelle's power, ringed her eyes. "Ben is outside. He'd like to join us. Help you look for... Jane Hawthorne?" Apparently,

Peggy could pick up thoughts from a vampire who wasn't even in the house.

Jasmine stiffened, dropping the telepath's hand and suddenly appearing beside the door to the rec room. "Benjamin Garrick?"

"Oh!" Peggy cried out, startled.

The vampire moved quickly. I could track her better than most because her undead energy was always present, dancing just out of my reach like Benjamin's.

"Um …" Peggy shook her head. "I guess so. He's … Ben in his own thoughts."

I tucked my knitting into my bag, keeping Ed with me as I crossed toward the door. I wasn't going to put my turtle within easy reach until Jasmine signed off on what Tony and Liam had planned. "I'll get him."

Jasmine raised her hand, palm facing me. She tilted her head as if listening. "How close is the vampire, Mory? Can you feel him?"

I glanced to Tony, then over at Liam. Everyone was watching me. "Not yet," I said stiffly. I wasn't particularly pleased about being put on the spot.

"Will he be safe among the fledglings?"

A chorus of *Hey!* and *Come on!* ensued behind us.

"We hang out every night," I said, becoming incensed.

Jasmine waved her hand dismissively. "Of course. I have no doubt of you."

A flush of pride tempered my anger, but I refused to be flattered when Jasmine was in the process of dissing Benjamin. "He'll be fine. I'm not certain about the detective, though."

Jasmine's head pivoted, taking in Liam. And though the gesture was decidedly inhuman, the sorcerer managed to hold his ground under her gaze. "Yes," the vampire said, still speaking to me. "This one is oddly prejudiced for one so young." Then she smiled scornfully. "A trait that will not survive long in the dowser's territory."

"Caution is not prejudice," Liam said.

Jasmine scoffed. "Let Benjamin know I am here, Mory. Before you invite him in. He might not want to meet me."

Peggy laughed, delighted. "Oh, he'll want to meet you, Jasmine. He likes to know everything. But not, like, in a know-it-all way. Right, Mory?"

I nodded, already heading for the back door.

"Stay out of the vampire's mind, Peggy," Liam said behind me. His tone suggested that he was completely exasperated by his adoptive sister.

"Vampires aren't usually so easy to read," Peggy said, her voice fading as I traversed the dark hall. "I can't read Kett at all, and only by touch with you, Jasmine."

"Peggy ..." Liam snarled a warning.

Gabby laughed.

I flicked on the exterior light as I opened the back door. I had already taken a step out when I spotted Benjamin crouched at the top of the concrete stairs. The overgrown backyard stretched out behind him, a series of tree- and bush-shaped shadows. It was already dark. And chilly.

"Hey, Benjamin."

He nodded, but his gaze was angled beyond me, through the open laundry room and down the hall. "Mory. I thought you might want my help this evening. But, uh ... who is that? I mean, I can, um ..."

Jasmine appeared behind me. One moment, I could feel her energy burbling on the other side of the house. Then it was behind me.

Benjamin stopped breathing, becoming completely still. Except for his eyes. His eyes widened, taking in every glorious golden inch that was Jasmine the vampire.

"Benjamin, son of Teresa Garrick, necromancer," I said, trying to not sound stiff and pissy.

"Child of Nigel Farris," Jasmine murmured, standing so close that her breath stirred my hair.

Benjamin nodded. Then he looked to me, silently prompting me to continue.

I cleared my throat, pushing past the dull ache trying to settle in my chest. "Jasmine. Child of Kettil, executioner and elder of the Conclave."

Benjamin smiled. I lowered my gaze to the concrete stairs. The genuine, welcoming warmth in his expression and the brush of magic that came with it weren't meant for me.

"Jasmine Fairchild?" he asked softly.

"Not anymore," she said matter-of-factly.

"But you look like her...Wisteria. A little. Same eyes."

"And when did you get such a good look at my cousin, vampire?" Jasmine asked teasingly. "When you were attempting to bite her in the graveyard?"

That pulled my attention back to Benjamin.

His smile faded. He wrapped his right hand over his left wrist. "I wasn't myself. Not as I am now. I was...starving. But I didn't know what...I wanted to eat. Or how."

Jasmine snorted.

I shuffled my feet, trying to ease the tension in my shoulders and back, but still keeping myself between Jasmine and Benjamin. Not that I could have stopped her if she went for him. The only thing I could really bank on was that hurting me to get to Benjamin would put the vampire on Jade's shit list. And very few Adepts would risk that.

Benjamin lifted his dark gaze, once again looking at Jasmine steadily over my shoulder. "You don't know what that's like? That hunger?"

I wasn't certain what he was asking. And the way Jasmine went thoughtfully still behind me, I wasn't sure she did either.

"I am Kett's," she said. "I ... haven't known hunger."

Benjamin tilted his head thoughtfully. "I see. Because he is ... powerful?"

"Do you regret it?" Jasmine asked, not bothering to answer Benjamin's question.

And suddenly, I felt like a complete outsider. Like I'd shoved myself into a very personal conversation.

"Not for one minute," Benjamin said. "You?"

I turned away, squeezing between Jasmine and the doorframe, then stepping back into the laundry area.

"No," Jasmine whispered. "Not for one second."

Still feeling like an intruder, I steadily crossed back toward the rec room, clutching Ed to my chest. I was behaving like an idiot, but thankfully, the vampires wouldn't notice.

"Necromancer," Jasmine called after me. "You are not to go anywhere with Liam Talbot without me."

I glanced back at her along the dark hallway. Her golden hair glowed softly in the overhead exterior light. Benjamin stood framed in the doorway with her, only a couple of inches taller but swathed in darkness.

"I don't trust him to put you first," Jasmine said.

"And you will?" I asked without thinking.

Jasmine smiled tightly. "As tasked by Jade ... and the executioner himself two nights ago. You and Rochelle are mine to protect."

I nodded, pushing open the rec room door and entering the room just to keep walking.

Tony spun around in his desk chair, triumphantly holding a tiny camera attached to an elasticized strap. "Ready for test number one."

I petted Ed as I crossed through the room. And as I did, I tried to ignore the weird feeling that I was leaving a part of myself behind me, with Benjamin and Jasmine on the basement stairs.

Three tests later, Jasmine and Tony had figured out how to get the camera to work on Ed while I had him walk around the room. Liam then raised the wards that coated the Talbot house, and Ed passed through them without trouble.

After that, the argument smoldering between Jasmine and Liam really ramped up. And while the sorcerer kept trying to speak to her in hushed tones in the hall, the vampire wasn't interested in excluding the rest of us from the discussion.

Being included should have been satisfying, since we so-called fledglings never were. But instead, it was a little boring sitting around waiting for a decision to be made.

Tony was still fiddling with Ed's camera while the turtle slowly shuffled around on his desk.

Jasmine's voice filtered in through the closed door. I picked up the words *elves*, *wards*, *orders*, and *protection*.

Liam's answer was simply a hissed sentence.

Benjamin snapped his notebook closed, gazing thoughtfully toward the closed door. "Jade didn't show."

"What?" I asked. "When?"

"This evening around five. We were actually supposed to meet yesterday, but I tried again today. It was my third attempt to reschedule our first interview."

I glanced over at Gabby. "When did you leave the bakery?"

"After closing. I took a nap after baking, then went back to help Peggy close. But yeah, no Jade all day. No Kandy. No witches, even."

I frowned. "No one showed up at all?"

"No one magical. Except me and Peggy." Gabby nudged her twin with her elbow.

Peggy shook her head, but her gaze remained remote. "Um, yeah, sure." She hadn't been listening. At least not to us.

My phone vibrated. And as I reached for it, I found myself desperately hoping it was a text from Jade.

"That's the best I can do from here," Tony said, pointing at my phone. "There's really no system or information to hack. I'm guessing files as far back as 1995 haven't been digitized."

I glanced at my screen, reading the text the tech sorcerer had just sent. The message consisted of a section number and a series of rows.

"I picked up older references to there once being a pauper's grave section at Mountain View. But I couldn't confirm it with any of the current information online, or even figure out if the practice has been maintained. But I'm fairly certain that a Jane Doe who died in Vancouver would have been buried there. And as best as I could figure out, their guidelines indicate that unclaimed remains are cremated and interred, but not within any specified timeline. They might have waited at least a year to see if anyone came forward with information on the body."

"Right." That all lined up with the information Rochelle had given me.

"So I narrowed down the interment dates to get you a possible location. I'm going to keep looking, but, uh … you know … I'm not really supposed to be hacking government sites."

"Thank you. That should be close enough."

"Compromised," Peggy murmured.

"What?" Gabby asked.

"That's what they're really fighting about out in the hall, Jasmine and Liam. What they're trying to not say out loud." Peggy's face was solemn. She leaned forward, speaking in a hushed tone. "Liam thinks Jade has been compromised. That she's … hurt. That she maybe even killed the others."

This wasn't news to me. But still, an extra layer of dread settled in my belly. Bravado only kept it at bay for short periods of time. "Yeah. He told me."

"All of them?" Gabby asked, shocked. "Everyone who's missing?"

"No," I said, trying to sound sure of myself. "Not the witches, or the oracle, or Jasmine, or any of us. And not Drake."

They all stared at me, shocked into silence.

"Listen," I said, my stomach churning with doubt. "It's going to be okay. This sort of thing happens around powerful people. We have a plan. It's going to be okay."

But I knew that doubt was creeping into my tone, because Benjamin stepped forward, laying his hand on my shoulder. And for some reason, what should have been a comforting touch made me angry.

"Standing around arguing about it endlessly is ridiculous." I pushed myself off the couch and marched over to the door, throwing it open.

Liam, standing with his back to me, flinched and whirled around. Jasmine, half hidden in the shadows at the base of the stairs, gazed at me steadily, not surprised by my sudden appearance.

"If Jade is in trouble, there's no question about trying to help her," I said.

Liam gestured toward me, looking pointedly at Jasmine.

"I'm not saying no," Jasmine said coolly. "I'm simply negotiating parameters. You will wait here with the others while Liam and I locate an easily defendable position. Then I'll ask Scarlett to provide a perimeter spell. And having Peggy around might be useful. Can she pick up the elves telepathically?"

"Absolutely not," Liam snarled. "I won't have my sister—"

Peggy and Gabby abruptly and eagerly appeared behind me in the doorway.

"I can totally help," Peggy said exuberantly. "The elf in Whistler gave off feedback."

"Peggy … not until—"

Gabby interrupted her older brother. "And if I'm there, I can amplify Mory, if needed. Or even help coordinate things with Peggy. We've been testing her range."

"Great," Jasmine said pertly. "We're almost settled, then."

"Almost?" Liam echoed sarcastically. "Would you like to wait until Bitsy gets home to put her in danger as well?"

Jasmine gave the detective a withering look. Then she smiled at me. Even Jade couldn't intimidate quite so effectively with only a smile. "Benjamin and I will be with Mory at all times."

"Benjamin?" Liam sneered. "He's not going to stand between Mory and an elf. Not for long, anyhow."

Jasmine shifted, suddenly standing too close to Liam. He flinched, but didn't back off. "No, Detective. That's your job. Benjamin will be there to grab Mory and run."

Liam clenched his jaw. But then he nodded curtly.

"What about Freddie?" I asked.

"What about Freddie?" Jasmine gave me a quelling look, telling me she clearly knew the shadow leech—but wanted to keep the information from the sorcerer.

I ignored the vampire's not-so-subtle implication that I should keep my mouth shut. Secrets weren't going to rescue Jade and the others. I wasn't certain we were, either. But it was past time to try.

"Who is Freddie?" Liam asked, folding his arms and glancing sternly between Jasmine and me.

"A shadow leech."

"What the hell is a shadow leech?"

"Freddie."

Liam swore under his breath.

I stifled a smirk.

Jasmine shook her head. "What about the leech?"

"Well, it ... he ... she consumes magic, right? Why not ask her to try to break through the elves' wards?"

"And can you summon it ... her?"

"Nope."

"Helpful, necromancer."

"You're very welcome."

Jasmine laughed quietly.

"Let me get this straight," Liam interjected. "There's some entity that eats magic just randomly roaming about Vancouver?"

I scoffed. "Not randomly. She hangs out with Jade."

"Jade," Liam echoed. "Jade, who is currently missing, controls some sort of magic eater?"

Jasmine shrugged. "Maybe Freddie is with her?"

"Um ..." I murmured. Freddie had seemed perfectly normal when she'd been playing around with my mother's bone collection. Though that didn't mean she wasn't in the know about what was going on with Jade. Too bad no one spoke shadow leech.

"Yes?" Liam asked pointedly, seemingly on the edge of snapping but holding himself in check.

"All good," I said pertly. "I'll ask Freddie next time I see her. Only instead of sitting around and doing nothing while you two figure out the particulars and get the spells from Scarlett, I'm heading up to Mountain View Cemetery—"

"Absolutely not," Liam growled. "This takes priority."

Jasmine raised her hand, hushing him. "For the oracle?"

I nodded, slightly peeved that Benjamin must have spilled the beans about Rochelle's request.

Jasmine glanced at Liam. "Ignoring a directive from an oracle isn't the best idea, sorcerer."

"I understood it wasn't time sensitive."

"Then why make the request at all? With everything else going on, why wouldn't Rochelle have waited?"

Liam shook his head. I was starting to feel a bit bad for him. He just wanted to be in control, in charge. He wanted to help. And we were all constantly shoving him back into place.

A curl of a smile softened Jasmine's face. "We are all just cogs in a big wheel, Detective. We take what magic brings us, and we try to do our best to sort through it."

Liam shook his head. "Witches, maybe. But sorcerers aren't so idle."

"What about vampires?" Jasmine whispered. "Shall we go hunting in the dark together, sorcerer?"

Liam swallowed, then nodded stiffly.

Jasmine grinned at me saucily. "I hear the detective has a great big gun that he's only allowed to use against hostiles."

"Who else would I shoot?" Liam asked huffily.

Jasmine shrugged belligerently, then she leaned toward me. "Text me if you need me. But keep Benjamin with you, yes?"

I nodded.

She brushed my shoulder with the tips of her fingers. "We'll find Jade, Mory. Liam was the last one to see her, so … if she's still where he thinks she is, and I deem it safe, then you'll use Ed and find her for us. But you'll wait for my text. You won't come looking for us until you hear from me. Okay?"

"Okay."

Jasmine turned away without another word, appearing suddenly at the end of the hall to open the back door.

Liam stepped into my space, leaning down to whisper, "Be careful with that vampire, Mory."

I scoffed. "What do you think he could do to a necromancer while in a graveyard, sorcerer?"

Liam met my gaze, nodding curtly. Then he grabbed a coat slung over the stair railing and followed Jasmine out of the house.

Borrowing Bitsy's older-model Jeep, Gabby, Peggy, Benjamin, and I drove up to Mountain View Cemetery. Then we proceeded to stumble around in the dark for a bit while I used a PDF map I'd found online to figure out what Tony meant by 'section.' By 'fourth row,' I assumed he meant the bottom, since those were the least expensive interment niches. And though it took a long while—to the extent that we actually would have been better off parking on the opposite side of the graveyard—we finally found the wall of the columbarium that I hoped was Rochelle's mother's final resting place.

Gabby and Peggy huddled off to one side. They were peering at the photo of the handwritten summoning spell that I'd taken a picture of earlier, then texted to Gabby in the SUV. As they did, they muttered between themselves.

I had mostly memorized the spell before falling asleep, then had reacquainted myself with the particulars during the drive—at least as much as I needed to. I pulled a white pillar candle out of my bag, lit it, and used it to try to read the names and dates on the niches.

"We need more candles," Gabby said.

"One will do." I turned back at the end of the first wall, scanning the two top rows on my way back, just in case I'd been wrong about how Tony had numbered them. "More will attract too much attention."

"From ghosts?" Peggy whispered, thrilled but slightly concerned.

"From the neighbors. My magic should shield me from casual observation, but I don't have the kind of power it would take to mask all of you as well. Or a bunch of light."

"Where's Ben?" Gabby asked.

Benjamin was walking the perimeter of the graveyard—though mentioning that I could feel his magic was more of a personal admission than I felt like making. "He'll be back. Why?"

"It says here, in the spell, that we need a…corpse for the soul to inhabit. If we want to talk to it. Ben is, um…I mean, he's kind of like a corpse, isn't he?"

"He's already using his body," I said wryly. Then, since Gabby and Peggy were both still staring at me, I elaborated. "Some necromancers use skulls and such to house the ghost they wish to speak to. For safety reasons."

"Safety?" Peggy echoed. "Talking to Rochelle's mom could be…dangerous?"

"Not to you. No."

"And to you?" Gabby was sounding strangely belligerent, as if she might have been thinking about withdrawing from the plan. And I was fairly certain that if I was going to pick up more than gender and possible age from the ashes of Rochelle's mother, I was going to need an amplifier.

My mother might have been dismissive of my power level. But she wasn't exactly wrong.

Sighing, I tugged my necklace out from underneath my sweater collar, careful to not snag the interior floats of yarn on the coins. "I don't need to confine a ghost or shade into a skull to keep it from attempting to…possess me—"

"Possess you!" Peggy cried.

I ignored her outburst. "Because Jade made me this." I let the necklace drop back against my upper rib cage. Its weight was comforting.

Gabby and Peggy eyed my necklace for a moment, then looked at each other—likely communicating telepathically.

"All right."

"Okay."

The twins spoke on top of each other, then turned their collective attention back to Gabby's phone.

Halfway along the second wall of the columbarium, I found dates in the early nineties—including three without inscriptions in 1995 and 1996, down in the bottom row. "Here we go." I crouched, set the candle at my feet, and brushed my fingers against the stone panels affixed to the front of the niches. With barely any effort, I reduced the three possibilities to the two that read as female.

"We need dirt from the grave of the soul we're trying to summon," Gabby said, disheartened. "Or … at least from the grave of an ancestor. We can't get either of those, can we?"

"Nope."

One of the females felt way older than the other, easily in her seventies when she'd died. Zeroing in on what I hoped was Jane Hawthorne's place of interment, I dug my keys out of my bag, along with a small tin that held my extra stitch markers. I emptied the rainbow-colored daisy markers back into the bag, then pressed the open container tightly against the bottom corner of the blank stone plaque.

"Sorry about this," I whispered. Then I used the key to a bike lock that I'd misplaced a couple of years ago to scrape against the plaque, as gently and discreetly as possible. A few flecks of stone fell into the tin. I stared at the paltry scrapings, already knowing it wasn't going to be enough—if it was even going to work as a replacement for grave dirt in the first place.

Defacing graves was hugely frowned upon among necromancers. Well, most necromancers. The kind that worked through official channels. Respect was everything when it came to wielding any sort of magic. So I had to hope that an oracle's request outweighed being disrespectful. I scrubbed the key against the stone more vigorously, gathering more flecks of stone.

When I was done, I quickly capped the container so that I didn't accidentally blow the flakes away. Then I settled down cross-legged in the damp grass that grew between the walls, placing my candle in front of the niche I'd defaced, about a foot and a half in front of me.

"The spell also said something about a pentagram," Gabby said quietly.

"A secondary barrier," I said. "Not necessary because I've already claimed this territory. But, um … I will ask you to join me." I gestured to my right.

Gabby tucked her phone in the pocket of her jacket, stepping forward and sinking to the ground beside me without hesitation.

"And me?" Benjamin asked, appearing to my left.

"If you can stay near, that would be great. But between you and Peggy, if you can just make sure no one wanders this way? I'm not sure I can split my attention between seeking out the shade and making sure that no one else is around."

"Cool."

"Sure." Peggy stepped up to Gabby's left. The four of us loosely formed a circle around the candle.

Gabby shoved the sleeves of her jacket and shirt up her forearms, then reached for me with both hands. I removed my arm warmers and pushed the sleeves of my sweater up, ignoring the instant chill across my bare wrists.

I reached for Gabby with my right hand, and she wrapped both of her hands around my wrist. The tin holding the scrapings was in the palm of my left hand, extending toward the candle and the niches.

"Do you need Peggy to read you the summoning spell?" the amplifier asked.

I shook my head. "The words don't matter … just the intention."

"Okay. Say when."

I closed my eyes, inhaling deeply. Then I opened my mind to the magic churning in the earth underneath and all around me. I exhaled, pushing away all the different strands of magic except the one tied to the tin I held in my left hand. "When."

Something tingled across my wrist. A shift of energy. Gabby's power. The strand connected to the tin grew in my mind, tying forward to the interment niche that held the remains of the younger woman.

Gabby's energy prickled up my forearm, then over my elbow, tickling me.

"Not too much," Peggy murmured.

"I remember the basement, thank you," Gabby grumbled. "Well... sort of."

A presence bloomed before me. A shadow in my mind's eye coming into being. "Jane Hawthorne," I whispered. The tin warmed in the palm of my hand—not hot enough to singe my skin, but more than simply a transference of my body heat. "Jane Hawthorne. I summon you in your daughter, Rochelle's, name. The oracle would speak to you."

The strand of magic tying the tin to the niches, to the shadowed presence, became more substantial. I channeled my power down it—the life force that was actually infusing the tin with warmth.

Gabby's energy tingled up over my shoulder. Then it suddenly stopped. She grunted, confused. "The necklace."

"It's all right," I whispered, directing all my attention to the presence that felt as though it was now crouched in front of me. "I think we've found her. Jane Hawthorne... oracle?"

A cold hand settled on my left shoulder.

I opened my eyes. Gabby, Peggy, and Benjamin hadn't shifted. The hand on my shoulder wasn't one of theirs.

I cinched the fingers of my right hand around Gabby's wrist so I wouldn't lose hold of her. I placed the tin down, then reached up to hover my hand over my left shoulder, over the hand I could still feel resting there.

"Jane?" I spoke the question to the shade I was fairly certain was crouched before me.

The presence grabbed my hand. Gabby gasped, presumably feeling some sort of feedback through our connection.

I struggled to keep my own heart rate under control, forcing myself to not pull my hand away. The strength of the contact might not have been an answer to my question. But for certain, it proved that I'd summoned more than simply an echo. Whatever—whoever—was touching me was more than a shade.

And maybe…maybe even more than a ghost? I had only felt such a solid connection once before.

With Rusty.

I had the sudden urge to stand, to have my feet firmly planted, before I continued to address whoever I'd summoned.

"I'm going to stand, okay?"

Gabby nodded. The ghost loosened her grasp and withdrew her hand. But as Gabby and I carefully got to our feet, still grasping each other's wrists, I kept hold of my connection to the presence I'd summoned.

Keeping the candle between me and the ghost, I allowed my connection to the tin to ebb, feeding more of my necromancy directly into the swirl of energy I could still feel rather than see. "Jane Hawthorne?"

A transparent woman appeared, standing before me. Smiling. She was taller than me, so taller than

Rochelle, but shorter than Benjamin where he stood to her left—and whose expression told me he couldn't see her at all. Her long straight white hair stirred in a breeze I couldn't feel. She wore a summer-weight blue dress that fell to below her knees, patterned with what I thought were flowers. But on closer inspection, they were black butterflies.

Rochelle had a black butterfly tattoo on her wrist.

The ghost of Jane Hawthorne also wore a thick-linked gold necklace with a large raw diamond. Rochelle's necklace.

All right, fine. I had inadvertently summoned Jane Hawthorne's ghost when I had simply hoped to verify her burial site. My mother would have been proud…or maybe totally livid. I could never be completely sure.

"I've been waiting for you, necromancer." Jane's voice echoed through my mind, her words meant only for me. Her accent was American, but mild enough that it was barely a hint. "I have something I need you to show my daughter."

"Yes, I'm sorry," I said. "I'll bring Rochelle. I didn't intend to summon you so thoroughly."

Gabby's hold on my wrist tightened.

"A ghost?" Benjamin asked, looking everywhere but the spot where Jane was actually standing.

"Yes…I …" Peggy hesitated. "I feel something…another presence. That's not possible, right? I mean, I shouldn't be able to hear the thoughts of a…ghost."

"I cannot wait any longer," Jane said sadly. "I must show you, Mory. You alone." She lifted her hand, reaching for me.

Allowing any contact between me and a summoned presence as strong as the one standing before me was a bad idea. For so many reasons. Including the fact that I hadn't introduced myself—Jane's ghost shouldn't have known my name.

Yet I raised my own hand, accepting her terms silently, so as not to confuse my companions.

The ghost stepped forward.

The candle flickered and died.

Gabby and Peggy started muttering back and forth between them. But I had eyes and ears only for Jane. I hadn't called for such a substantial presence since the time Rusty had returned to me.

Jane's fingers passed through mine. She frowned. "Necromancer," she said. "This is of utmost importance."

"Tell me," I said. "I'm listening."

She shook her head. "It cannot be translated into words."

My heart rate ratcheted up. This was an exceptionally bad, bad, bad idea. The dowser was going to kill me.

I reached up, opening the clasp on my necklace with the hand that Gabby didn't have in a death grip.

"What are you doing, Mory?" Benjamin asked.

"Hold this for me?"

"No. No way. You're supposed to keep it on."

"Ben." I held the necklace out to him, keeping all my attention on Jane. "Hold this for me. Put it back on if I seem to be in trouble."

Jane smiled sadly. "I wish you no ill will. No ill effects. But this must be done."

Benjamin took the necklace from me.

I reached for Jane. Her hand became solid in mine.

Gabby and Peggy gasped. Benjamin went very still. I gathered that they could now see the ghost holding my hand.

"It will take but a moment," Jane whispered. Then without any other warning, she stepped toward me.

She stepped into me.

I gasped as all the air was pressed from my lungs. I stifled a cry as I momentarily lost control of my body. I looked at my outstretched hand, but I could no longer move it.

Then magic welled underneath my feet. A fierce torrent of power. I'd never felt anything remotely similar. A white wash of energy flowed up through me, racking my body, wiping my mind.

I tried to scream but I had no voice. I tried to fall but I had no body. I tried to think but... I saw instead.

I saw.

Images flooded my mind... elves and swords and demons and blood and a young girl, maybe eight years old, with light-brown skin and white hair. She was in the middle of it all.

I saw.

A city in ruins. Death roaming the streets. Chaos unleashed.

I saw.

Everything.

Then... nothing.

A sea of blinding white.

A moment of nothing.

Jane stepped away from me.

I stumbled. Gabby and Benjamin grabbed my elbows and kept me on my feet. Peggy was clutching her head.

"What... what ..." I was crying, tears streaming down my cheeks. My hands were shaking in terror.

Jane took my hand in her own. "I'm sorry. But what needed to be done is done now, necromancer."

"That's too much... I can't even remember half of it. I... I... can't remember any of it."

Jane nodded. "No need for you to remember. Now that you've seen, my daughter will see."

I wiped my face with my free hand. "Like how? She'll read my mind?"

Jane shook her head, her expression full of regret. "That is not how our power works. I have released the visions. They will find their way to Rochelle."

"Find their way … that seems like wishful thinking. This is too important. You must speak with your daughter."

The energy filling Jane—my energy—began to fade. I suddenly felt drained, epically tired. I struggled to fortify my connection to her through our still-connected hands, but she was becoming more and more transparent.

"I must go."

"Please. I'll bring Rochelle back."

"No. I would not have her see me this way. I waited for you, but now I must move on … there is more …"

Jane's mouth continued to move, but her words were unintelligible. Something was keeping her from talking.

She was speaking of something that magic … or whatever you wanted to call it … didn't want me to hear.

"Tell Rochelle you couldn't find me."

"I'm not going to lie, lady."

Jane laughed. "Then tell her I see her. Tell her I love her. I don't regret anything other than the moments we didn't get to spend together. Tell her I see her. I saw her for years and years before she was even mine. She'll understand."

"I see her," I repeated.

"Yes. Thank you." Then Jane faded away.

One moment, I could feel her essence. The next, she was gone. Off to one of those other levels of existence.

"She's gone," Peggy whispered, dropping her hands to her sides. "Jane. So much … love …"

"Did you … hear? Do you remember?"

Peggy shook her head.

Benjamin settled my necklace around my neck.

"That wasn't a ghost," I whispered, reaching up and touching the lowest coins where they felt heavy against my breastbone.

"What do you mean?" Benjamin asked.

I shook my head, unable to answer. Unable to articulate the feeling or the idea that Jane Hawthorne had somehow managed to tie herself, her spirit … her soul to this plane of existence. Then she had waited for me to reach out to her. Because she'd died before she had the chance to articulate the vision she'd just somehow channeled through me?

The idea of that even being possible was staggering, overwhelmingly inconceivable … and I was a necromancer. I dealt with death. I might not make a living at it yet, but I would eventually. "Soul magic," I murmured.

Peggy wrapped her arm around my shoulders. "Let's go back to your place while we wait to hear from Liam and Jasmine, hey? It's closer. If we ask nicely, Gabby might make us brownies. We're going to need the fuel."

Gabby grunted. "I'll need ingredients."

I allowed the twins to draw me away, looking back only as we hit the path.

Benjamin was lingering by the columbarium, jotting notes in his notebook. "Coming, Ben?"

He nodded absentmindedly. "I think a witch might be able to fix the scratches on the stone. And the oracle will want to have the plaque properly engraved. I've noted its exact location."

"Thank you. I'll ask Burgundy. And mention it to Rochelle."

He tucked the notebook away in his bag, picked up the candle and tin I had unintentionally abandoned, and sauntered after us.

Still completely drained, I forced myself to text Rochelle from the back seat of the Jeep, being as concise as possible. I could elaborate in person.

I found your mom.

She said to tell you that she 'sees you.' She said you'd know what she means.

But she won't be coming back. She's moved on.

And she did something. Something about releasing a vision.

I suspect you might know about that already.

Message sent, I snoozed. Benjamin was bent over his notebook in the seat beside me, his black-inked handwriting filling page after page. In the front seats, Peggy chatted quietly with Gabby as she drove.

I was okay. I would have to ask Peggy later what exactly she'd picked up from Jane's spirit—if anything. And I wasn't certain how up front I wanted to be about allowing the spirit of an oracle to possess me. But since my mother never bothered to question me, and since everyone else was either missing in action or worried about those missing in action, I doubted the subject would come up.

Either way, I'd broken a cardinal rule by removing my necklace. But thankfully, I appeared to still be alive. I was completely certain that was due to Jane Hawthorne's intentions, though, not my own abilities. I wasn't going to be repeating the activity soon, if ever.

We were a block from my house when my phone pinged. I glanced at the screen, expecting a text from Rochelle. It was Jasmine.

>*Ready for you. Meet me by the statue of the running guy. Bring Ben and the twins.*

Terry Fox.

>*Sure. Whoever. Let me know when you're near. I'll come get you.*

We're about fifteen minutes away.

"Hey," I said. "Liam and Jasmine are ready for us."

Peggy turned around in her seat, blinking her big blue eyes in my direction. "Operation rescue mission is a go?"

"Undead turtle reconnaissance is a go. Assuming I can get Ed through the elves' wards. And even if I can, it's not like he can drag Jade out of the stadium."

"That part will get worked out, Mory." Peggy smiled softly. "Still, it'll be nice to be doing the rescuing. We've never been on that side of a situation before."

"Yeah. I hear you."

I pulled Ed out of my satchel, holding him against my chest as I settled back against the seat and closed my eyes. I was fairly certain we were nowhere near whatever the finale was going to be with the elves. Fallen warriors or no fallen warriors. But even getting ten minutes sleep would help me face whatever was coming.

Rochelle

Buzz.

The city of Vancouver was laid to waste. Ruined. Swathed in harshly edged charcoal grays, smoldering, crumbled buildings spread from the shoreline to the mountains. Not a speck of green among the fallen towers.

Buzz.

I twisted my ankle in the concrete rubble, stumbling but managing to not fall and impale myself on the twisted rebar that jutted out everywhere. I wasn't quite sure where I was standing. I wasn't quite sure I was actually in the city at all.

Buzz.

A whisper of darkness slipped up my spine, chilling me through and through. A presence loomed behind me. A dreadful echo of the section of my soul I thought I'd walled off. A future I had hoped I'd thwarted.

I slowly pivoted, already knowing what I would see perched on the towering pile of rubble rising to my right. I wrapped my right hand tightly over my left, crushing my fingers in my grasp, covering the diamond-speckled wedding ring I wore. My mind screamed for me to look away, to look anywhere else.

Buzz.

I was wrong. I had expected the demon with its glowing crimson eyes, viciously sharp teeth, and wickedly curved talons. And the black-scaled beast was there, perched on a pile of steel girders, concrete, and glass...so, so much shattered glass everywhere. Knee high in some places.

It was the girl I hadn't expected.

She was slim and tall, around eight or nine. Her tousled white hair hung halfway down her back, raggedly hacked off at the ends as though she'd cut it herself. Dressed head to toe in mismatched shades of gray, she practically blended in with the crumbling concrete. Except for her hair and the demon by her side.

The girl reached up and scratched the black beast underneath its chin. It curled its spiked tail around her ankles and purred.

The sound ground into my bones. I shuddered, gasping.

The demon swiveled its broad, flat head, pinning me with flaming eyes.

Rochelle. Its voice screeched through my mind. *My Rochelle.*

The girl spun to face me, crouching beneath the demon's chest as if she expected the creature to protect her. As if it were hers.

As if it were her demon, not mine.

Her skin was light brown. Her features were desperately familiar. But it was her eyes that made me lightheaded. Her eyes were brilliant white.

The white of oracle magic.

My magic.

My heart stopped beating, even as it somehow crammed itself into my throat.

The girl wore a silver whip twined around her waist. The whip that had belonged to my grandmother,

Win. The whip I was fairly certain was currently in the sorcerer Blackwell's possession.

The whip that was supposed to have been mine to wield.

The girl's whited-out gaze flicked around, looking everywhere at once but seeing nothing.

"Mom?" she whispered.

She couldn't see me.

I wasn't standing there at all.

"Mom?!"

Buzz.

My phone was buzzing.

With text messages.

I was dreaming.

No...I was having a vision.

I opened my eyes.

I was in the living room, where I had fallen asleep on the couch. Beside me, Beau was snoring quietly, his head tilted back at a harsh angle.

The white of the vision threatened to take my sight, and I almost let it. I almost allowed my insistent magic to overwhelm my rational mind. Because of the girl. Because I wanted to see her. Again and again.

Instead, I focused on the present, settling my hands across my swollen belly and listening to Beau breathe. I felt the firmness of my taut skin through my T-shirt. And knowing that my baby slumbered curled within me edged the vision farther away, clearing my eyesight until all I saw was the dimly lit living room. The TV was on, still playing whatever movie Beau had been watching when he must have fallen asleep after me. I took a deep breath, gently rubbing my belly and the child slowly growing within, still three months from being ready for this world.

My baby. Beau's and mine.

My child…with my demon, my whip, in a future destroyed.

I squeezed my eyes closed. It wasn't the time to shut down. It wasn't the time to make guesses, to jump to conclusions. I knew better.

"Beau," I whispered.

Beau stood. One moment he was asleep, then he was standing over me and awake. Ready for anything.

"I need to draw," I said, reaching up with both hands so he'd help me off the couch.

"Is it bad?" he asked.

I met his dark aquamarine gaze. Desperate to keep the terror threatening to pull me under at bay, I could only nod.

It was bad.

"Jade?" he asked.

I shook my head. But then I paused, thinking of the ruined city. Thinking of the vision I'd had of Jade two nights before and of the feeling of being desperately angry but utterly lost that had come with it.

— Oh, God.

"Maybe," I whispered.

Maybe it was Jade. Maybe whatever was going on with Jade was going to destroy the city, was going to alter the future so…so…that my child was guarded by a demon without me…or Beau.

Since the vision that had partially manifested at the dance club, I'd seen nothing. Nothing of Jade. Not after seeing her surrounded by mist, lost in the deep, dark fog. Unreachable. And no sign of any of the other Adepts that called Vancouver home. Not even when I'd touched Mory in the cemetery yesterday. I had actively tried to read the necromancer and gotten … more of that nothing.

And in that nothingness, I thought I might be looking toward my own death. A death I couldn't see, wouldn't see coming. Unless … unless I could see it by seeing my child … abandoned, perhaps even orphaned, in a ruined city …

Tears slipped down my cheeks and I started to shake. My breath was coming fast and hard. I was panicking. Panic wasn't helpful. Tears solved nothing. But … I … I …

Beau gripped my shoulders. "Tell me. Tell me, love. Let me help."

"Beau … Beau …" I reached for him, clutching him, feeling his strength and finding my own. The baby shifted in my belly, nestled between us.

"We'll fix it," Beau murmured, slowly caressing my hair. "That's why you see. So we can fix it."

I nodded against his chest. I didn't know enough to panic yet. I had more to see. "I'm going to need a new sketchbook."

Instead of breaking contact with me, Beau swept me up in his arms. Carrying me through the house that was too large for just the two of us, he climbed the stairs and brought me to my studio.

I settled at the desk at the window that overlooked the chicken coop, rather than going to the easel I used for large-scale sketches. In between car projects and helping out with renovations, Beau had spent the year prepping and fencing a garden area that was going to surround the main coop and run. He had just finished building a grow-out coop for chicks we'd hatched in late October. They were almost ready to come out of the brooder in the garage.

Pulling a new set of charcoals out of the middle desk drawer, I had to angle my body to get close enough to rest my left elbow on the desk. Beau set a fresh sketchbook in front of me. I reached out and touched his hand before he could withdraw it, taking further comfort in his warmth and the firmness of his skin. He was real. He was present. My present. And together, we would tackle the future.

"Beau," I whispered, looking up to meet his gaze. "She … she's magnificent."

He knelt, pressing his hand across my belly. "She? Our daughter?"

"Yes. I think so. Around nine years old …"

Beau swallowed harshly, realizing that whatever I'd seen, whatever had wrenched such an unusual emotional display from me—my second in as many days—had to do with our daughter.

Two nights before, I'd seen something having to do with the dowser, Jade Godfrey, while we'd been celebrating her bachelorette party and the elves had shown up in force. But I wasn't able to articulate the vision. I couldn't even draw it—the dowser trapped in an endless fog, somehow captured by some unknown power … and filling me with a fear of the elves' gemstones that I still didn't understand. It didn't make any sense. Not at the time the vision hit, and not any time since. Not even when I'd sat with a blank page before me and charcoal in my hand for hours as soon as I'd gotten home, safely ensconced behind wards that had been erected to protect me.

And now this vision of the nine-year-old girl with Beau's face, my magic—and a ruined city around her. And protected by the demon? My demon.

The white mist that preceded every vision threatened the edges of my peripheral vision.

Leaving one hand on my belly, Beau cupped his other hand to my face. "We'll do whatever it takes." He looked grim, determined. "Promise me, Rochelle. Whatever it takes."

"Yes. Whatever it takes. Whatever the cost."

He cleared his throat, stopping himself from asking more. He'd see the details in black and white soon enough. "I'll get you some water."

"Thank you."

He rose, brushing a kiss against my forehead.

I turned back to the desk, flipping the sketchbook open and pressing fresh charcoal to the first page.

Effortlessly, the white of my oracle magic flooded forward at my bidding, enveloping my mind, taking my sight.

And I drew.

I drew the future. And with every stroke, every smudge, curve, and hard edge, I swore to unmake it.

Destiny be damned.

Whatever it took. Whatever the cost.

By the time the grip of the vision had eased, it was the deep dark of early morning outside my window. It wasn't all that cold out, but I found myself wishing for a reason to build a fire and hunker down, hide away from the world.

From the battle for the future.

A war that might have already started—and that might already have been way beyond my ability to shape.

I slumped back in my chair. Beau peeled out of the darkness to my right. He'd been sitting on the love seat, waiting to feed me. To make sure I was okay.

And I was. Just shaky.

"What time is it?" I asked.

"About 2:00 A.M." He held out a plate of sliced apple, and I eagerly plucked one off the plate.

It wasn't really a good time of year for apples, but Beau had built a cold storage space in the unheated garage that currently also housed the chicks and two of his project cars. It helped the apples keep longer. Back in October, he had taken me—along with a toy wagon he'd borrowed from our neighbors' children—to the UBC Apple Festival, where he'd proceeded to buy me a half-dozen of every variety they offered while I laughed at all the stares his indulgence had drawn. Normally, it was his looks that drew attention. But that sunny afternoon, it had been an epic mound of apples in a sturdy plastic wagon that had everyone amused.

"Mmm," I said, nibbling on a slice of a yellow-skinned, creamy-fleshed apple appreciatively. "Aurora Golden Gala. I think this might be my favorite."

Beau knelt down next to me, reaching up to tuck my hair behind my ear. "I know. I have three trees on order from the nursery already. I was going to tell you on your birthday."

I wrapped my hand around the back of his neck, curling forward to press my forehead against his. "Beau …"

He pressed another piece of apple into my free hand, even though my fingers were caked in charcoal. "I also ordered a Gala, a Salish, a Granny Smith, and an Ambrosia."

"That's a lot of apple trees. Way more than we discussed."

"They're all dwarf or semidwarf. So high yield but smaller trees. I haven't been able to source a Rubinette or a Belle de Boskoop yet. The Thompsons might be able to help. At least with sourcing some scion wood from Summerland. I know you liked the Boskoop for making applesauce."

"That's the apple Jade used for her first batches of *Clarity in a Cup*." The dowser, who owned and ran a bakery when she wasn't facing off against elves and getting trapped in some sort of endless fog in my visions, had created a cupcake that reminded her of the way my magic tasted to her.

I savored the apple as I chewed, and allowed myself to wonder if the oracle magic that the girl in my vision wielded would taste the same to Jade as mine did. Except if the future I'd just sketched came to pass... well, I couldn't imagine that Jade was going to be alive to see it.

I squeezed my eyes shut.

Beau brushed a soft kiss against my forehead as he murmured soothingly, "I'm going to plant the apples all around the coops. And when they grow a bit and branch out, you can free-range the chickens without worrying so much about hawks and eagles."

I let out a shuddering breath. Then I took and ate another slice of apple from the plate. "Okay... okay."

"And I think we should add a couple of plum trees and maybe pear? We can talk about varieties."

"Okay." I straightened in my seat, snagging another piece of apple from the plate. Then I turned my attention to my sketchbook. It was still open to the last page. I flipped it closed. The edges of the paper were dark with smudged charcoal fingerprints. I looked down at my hands. My skin was evenly blackened almost to my wrists. "Did you look?"

"You know I didn't."

I nodded.

"Mory has been texting."

"Okay."

"I'm going to warm you some apple juice." He straightened, turning to leave.

"No, wait. I'm ... I'm not sure we have the time."

Beau paused, waiting in the darkness.

I didn't know what to say. I felt drained. Visions didn't usually come with timelines attached, but I somehow knew we had to keep moving forward. Quickly.

"A nap at least, Rochelle. Please. For the baby."

Hot tears spiked at the edges of my eyes.

Beau was instantly cradling my face in his hands. "I'm sorry. I'm sorry. I know ... I know ... I didn't mean to suggest ... "

I pushed against his hands, getting close enough to brush a kiss across his lips. He closed the embrace immediately. Pulling me into his lap so I was straddling him, drawing me as close as he could while we were still wearing clothing. I opened all my senses to him, darting my tongue in his mouth, relishing in his warmth, in the taste of him, in the strength of his arms.

Cupping my ass in one hand, he brushed his fingers up my spine, then cradled my head in his other hand.

I pulled back from the kiss, wanting to simply look at him, caressing his beautiful face. "She looks like you," I whispered. "But ... with my ... eyes. The color, anyway."

A bright, brilliant smile of pure happiness spread across Beau's face, and he kissed me with quiet joy. "We'll make it okay, Rochelle. Whatever is going to happen."

"We'll try. The future is fluid, but—"

Beau kissed me again, stopping me from completing the rest of the phrase I'd picked up from my mentor, the far seer of the guardian dragons.

... *destiny is immutable.*

"You said she's nine in the vision, so we have time."

"You know that's not how it works," I whispered. Part of me just wanted to stay in his arms, slowly removing articles of clothing and making love as the sun rose. But another part understood that I had to start confronting what I'd seen. "Something is happening now. I think it's tied to Jade somehow."

"Did you see the dowser?"

I shook my head. Using Beau's shoulders to help me to my feet, I turned to flip open the sketchbook on the desk to a random middle page. The revealed sketch was roughly rendered, almost frantic. I would need to go back through the book guided by my magic, refining the drawings that called for it. But, outlined in smudged charcoal, the girl, the demon, and the whip were clearly discernible.

"Same demon?" Beau asked. His tone was low and raw.

"Yes."

"Same whip?"

"Yes."

"Blackwell has the whip."

"As far as we know."

Beau scrubbed his hand across his face. I wasn't the only one who hadn't really slept yet. "So the sorcerer is involved."

"I...I...don't know. In this future?" I tapped the sketch. "Yes, obviously the whip must come to the girl somehow. But how it ties into our present? I don't know. I have to go back through, looking for clues."

"Can you do that after a nap?"

I glanced up at him, though I really couldn't see him well in the dark. If I said no, then Beau would respect my decision. But facing whatever we were about to face at six months pregnant and on no sleep wasn't ideal. And if my magic was giving me a reprieve, I ought to take it.

I wordlessly held my hands out to him. He gently tugged me toward the door, then led me down the hall to our bedroom.

I had forgotten to check the text messages from Mory. That was what I was thinking as I woke from a heavy slumber. But it was the magic causing all the hair on my arms to stand on end that had actually pulled me from my sleep.

I sat up, gathering the sheets and duvet to my chest. Energy rolled across my skin again, but my tattoos remained inert.

Not my magic, then. Not my oracle or my sorcerer power.

Wakened by my movement, Beau slipped out of the bed, padding silently across the room and opening the curtains ever so slightly. A sliver of diffused starlight slashed across his face. The clouds that had covered the sky the past few days must have thinned.

The magic rolled across my arms again. This time, with a little more edge. And I finally recognized it from the tests Scarlett Godfrey had run us through three separate times. I'd thought her caution was overkill. Because who would ever try to step on our property without our permission?

I had obviously been wrong.

How wrong? That remained to be seen.

"The outer wards," I murmured.

Security wards, put in place by Pearl Godfrey and her daughter, Scarlett, ran the entire perimeter of the two properties Beau and I had bought almost a year and a half ago. Then the witches had added even stronger secondary wards around the main house. Both sets of wards were always in place, always active, because neither Beau or I wielded the kind of magic that could raise or maintain them.

"Someone is trying to break through?" I asked. "To gain access to the property?"

Someone magical, it went without saying. Because only the magically inclined triggered the protections. Tess and Gary lived on the second property, and had a constant stream of friends over for tea or dinner without a single incident.

"Feels like it." Beau reached for and pulled on a pair of sweatpants.

"Why would they come here?" I whispered, already knowing that there were two possible answers to my question. Already remembering that two evenings before, Kett had coolly informed Jasmine that an oracle was more important than he or she could ever be. He was the executioner and an elder of the vampire Conclave, which sounded crazy important. And Jasmine was his child.

"The witches' grid," Beau said, pulling on a T-shirt that stretched across his chest.

That was the second possible reason—and the primary reason for the heavy magical wards encasing both the property and the house. The witches' grid that currently spread across all Vancouver was anchored at the main house. Because of me. It was the witches' way of tying me and my oracle power into their magical detection system.

Beau reached for me, softly brushing my cheek with his fingers. "They won't get through."

We didn't bother articulating who 'they' were. We didn't need to.

Elves. There was no one else that it could have been. Possibly the same elves that Jade had faced off against two nights before. And with no one having heard from the dowser as far as I knew, the elves were now attempting to compromise the witches' grid. Or worse ...

"I won't let them take you, Rochelle." Beau shook his head slightly, correcting himself. "You won't let them take you."

"Or you," I murmured.

He kissed me, then stepped away, practically appearing at the door in the same motion. "I'm going to get Gary and Tess. Text Pearl, please."

More magic shifted. My magic. "Wait," I breathed, reaching for Beau. "Wait."

He stepped back, taking both my hands, then kneeling before me formally. "What do you see, oracle?"

I waited. We waited.

But nothing more happened.

My magic abated.

"Not yet," I said. "Whatever is coming, whatever more I'm supposed to see. It's ... not ready yet."

"Something we have to do first, perhaps. To trigger whatever you're supposed to see," Beau murmured, pressing a kiss to each of my hands. "I'll be right back."

Then he was gone.

I climbed off the bed, pulling the duvet with me as I crossed to the window. I watched as Beau slipped from the back of the house and crossed the yard toward the second property, where Gary and Tess had nearly finished building their own house. The exterior paint and landscaping had to wait for warmer weather, though.

It had actually taken longer to find the adjoining properties in Southlands, convince the neighbors to sell, then liquidate enough of my inheritance to pay for it all than it had for Beau and me to be legally adopted by Gary and Tess. That adoption process had involved a lot less paperwork, as well. We had set the four of us up as co-owners of both properties, as a simple outward declaration of our relationship. And not even Pearl Godfrey had batted an eyelash when I'd introduced her to my new nonmagical parents. Though I suspected that the elder witch had been so eager to get her hands on the penthouse in False Creek that my mother had left me that she'd probably have gone along with any plan that involved selling it.

I couldn't see my chicken coop from the bedroom window. Beau had situated it in view of my studio because I spent most of my time there. Willing myself to stay calm, I closed my eyes and imagined him in the spring, planting the apple trees he'd ordered. I imagined the chickens roaming underneath their green leaves …

Then I got dressed.

Because simply wishing for things never made them happen.

Not for me, anyway.

I picked up my phone to text Pearl, but got delayed by the series of text messages still waiting for me from Mory. And her quick, almost emotionless overview of what had transpired in the cemetery the previous night stopped me in my tracks.

I read it again, this time putting it together with the vision that had hit me when I'd fallen asleep on the couch a few hours earlier. And the understanding of the connection between those two events made me so queasy that I was forced to hover over the toilet in the en suite, waiting until wave after wave of terror had cooled on my skin.

Then I forced myself to read Mory's text messages a third time.

>*I found your mom.*

>*She said to tell you that she 'sees you.' She said you'd know what she means.*

>*But she won't be coming back. She's moved on.*

>*And she did something. Something about releasing a vision.*

> *I suspect you might know about that already.*

I squeezed my eyes shut, fighting another pulse of terror and a sudden, desperate wish that I could contact Chi Wen as easily as I could send a text message.

But what would my all-seeing mentor tell me? That magic made everything possible. Even my dead mother's ghost releasing a vision for me to see, to sketch, to try to thwart. He would say that I had choices. And that additional possible paths would open up as I made decisions.

I closed the lid on the toilet. Then I texted Pearl. Whoever was overseeing the grid might have already spotted the elves' attempt to break through our wards, so I didn't bother being verbose.

Elves here. We're in the house. I'll text if we need help.

Then I forced myself to shove my phone in my hoodie pocket, and get the lockbox full of premade spells from the safe in our walk-in closet.

I would tackle the full impact of Mory's revelations after the elves had been dealt with.

Beau had herded Tess and me into the mostly un-used—and therefore, sparsely furnished—front living room. Gary had made a break for the kitchen, where I could hear him happily grumbling to himself as he tried for the umpteenth time to make sense of our coffee maker. Tess, hastily dressed in skinny-legged jeans and a bulky sweater that fell to her knees, finished fussing over wrapping a colorful knit blanket around my legs. Then she curled up on the stiff-backed couch next to me, tucking her pink-pedicured toes underneath my thigh. Beau hadn't given her time to grab socks, and she refused to wear shoes in the house. Her curly hair—streaked with gold and silver—tumbled around her face.

The outer wards fell.

Energy flushed across my skin, then disappeared with an audible snap. The black butterfly tattoo on my left inner wrist stirred, confirming that something magical was now stalking across my property. I pressed my right hand over it, then raised my gaze to Beau.

His eyes blazing the green of his shapeshifter magic, Beau turned from the window where he'd been keeping watch. His gaze fell to my hands, knowing almost as well as I did what I was trying to deny, what the black butterfly represented magically. The identification of magical things or people—or occasionally, a sense of where my magic needed to be applied or focused.

"Stay here," I said. "With us." Except I knew he wouldn't, that he couldn't, even before the demand left my lips.

"What's wrong?" Tess asked, glancing back and forth between us.

"The outer wards have fallen." I struggled to get my legs untucked from the blanket Tess had swathed me in. "At least, I think that's what it was."

"Yes." Beau crossed out of the front room, heading back through the house.

I grabbed the box of spells from the coffee table, following him with Tess on my heels.

"Gary!" Tess called as we passed the entrance to the kitchen. Her gray-haired, barrel-chested husband appeared to have fallen asleep by the coffee maker—though by the aroma filling the kitchen, he'd gotten it set up and turned on before closing his eyes. "The kids are going outside!"

Gary snapped awake.

"Not both of us." Beau turned back at the end of the hall, just before the open door to the mudroom that exited into the backyard. He cradled my face in his hands. "Listen to me, Rochelle."

"No."

"Stay here, guard the house. For Tess and Gary. For the baby. Nothing is going to happen."

"Fine. If nothing happens, I'll stay in the house."

"Damn it, oracle," Beau muttered. He pressed a not-so-gentle kiss to my lips, then released me to step into the mudroom and pull off his T-shirt.

Tess's hands fell on my shoulders, holding me to her. I clutched the box of spells and tried to keep my face from revealing how terrified I was.

"Beau?" Gary asked from the hall. "No police, then?"

Beau shook his head, offering our adoptive father a tight smile. He stripped off his jogging pants and opened the back door.

"Text Pearl again," he said. "Lock this door behind me."

"Of course," I said. "Remember…remember …"

"I always do." Then Beau stepped from the house, his shifter magic rolling around him in a torrent of power.

Gary brushed by Tess and me, closing and locking the door. I nodded my thanks, but turned and quickly crossed through the house so I could look out the front window.

My phone vibrated in my pocket. I pulled it out to find a message from Pearl.

>*The property wards have fallen. Stay in the house. I'll send Scarlett.*

I texted back.

Beau has gone out to investigate. I'll text when we know what's going on.

Without waiting for a reply, which was likely just going to be more orders that neither Beau or I were going to heed, I tucked my phone in my hoodie pocket and opened the lockbox. A series of painted and carved stones, sorted by color and tucked into a foam insert, lay within its steel walls. Premade witch spells, ready to be used and triggered by anyone. They were dangerous—hence keeping them locked up tight and in the safe for good measure.

Not thinking about what was going to happen next, I systematically began to place the spells on the windowsill before me. The future would reveal itself without my urging.

"Rochelle?" Tess asked. "Have you…have you seen what is about to happen?"

"Not yet." I cleared the wedge of fear from my throat. "Now…you remember what Scarlett said about these spells?"

"They are ... live. So even Gary or I can use them."

"Yes. But carefully. Blue for deflection spells, say if you're in the process of running. Yellow for invisibility spells ..."

"We can't be moving if we want to use those ... for cover."

"Right. And red for offensive spells." I brushed my fingers over the four red-painted rocks in the collection. "You only throw them as a last resort. If the elves get in the house. If ... if Beau and I are ... down. And you'd better be running away when you do."

Tess curled her hand over mine. "We aren't leaving you."

"I know." I glanced over at her. "But someday, we might have to leave you."

She smiled, tears in her eyes. "That's how it always is, with parents and children. But not today. Okay?" She glanced over at her husband.

Gary stepped up behind us. He'd pulled a base-ball bat out of the front closet—a bat that was for me, placed there by Beau. Another weapon that I wouldn't accidentally hurt myself with. But a bat or the tactical pen I carried in my satchel weren't going to work against elves.

Not if the reason they were here was because they'd already killed Jade.

Fear clogged my throat again, and I struggled futilely to swallow it away. There really wasn't any other explanation. There was no other reason or way that elves would be coming for me, unless Jade had fallen.

I twisted my wedding ring on my finger, keeping my gaze steady out of the front window.

Waiting. Waiting.

Either for circumstance or for magic to tell me which way to move. Because I believed. I believed that there was a reason I saw. I couldn't control other people's choices, not with absolute certainty. But I believed that the vision of my child wouldn't have come to me—especially not in the way Mory had described—unless I could thwart it.

So I waited to see which way magic moved me.

Two elves slowly approached the house—dragging Beau in his half-human, half-werecat form across the lawn. I couldn't tell if he was alive from my vantage point at the front window. Harsh pain squeezed my chest, constricting my heart, and I slammed my left hand against the glass standing between me and my love, my reason for being.

Magic crackled, running down my arm. My barbed-wire tattoo shivered as if waking. Then it bristled. My power flowed from me into the glass, then rippled out across the wards covering the house.

This display drew the attention of both elves in the yard. They adjusted their approach, stopping about twenty-five feet from the house and dropping Beau to the ground.

Tess moaned.

I kept my gaze on Beau, looking for a sign. A sign of life. Or confirmation of his death.

Though I already knew that my response was going to be the same either way.

The elves scanned the house, most likely assessing the layers upon layers of magic that coated it. Then they settled on staring at me. Pale skinned, green eyed, and easily over six and a half feet tall, they were dressed as I'd seen them in the dance club—wearing white armor that looked like hard plastic but appeared to be somehow flexible. Their skin glowed in the filtered starlight. They were both carrying swords that appeared to have been carved out of green-tinted ice or murky glass.

The elf on the right was cradling his left arm across his chest. The face, neck, and chest of the one on the left was scored by black slashes. It was an easy guess that their wounds had been inflicted by Beau.

Energy I could see but not feel from behind the wards shifted. As it did, Beau transformed into his human visage.

The elves stumbled a step to either side, then stilled, waiting for an attack that didn't come. Beau lay curled on his side. Naked. And wounded enough that his magic had forced the transformation on him, even while unconscious.

But he was still alive.

The pain in my chest eased, replaced with a cool, detached ache.

The elves closed the space between themselves and Beau again. The one on the left flicked his sword downward, making it somehow lengthen before my eyes. Then he laid it across Beau's neck. Both elves regarded me steadily with their dispassionate, glistening green eyes.

I laughed. The sound was terrible even to my own ears. "They shouldn't have come at night."

"No, Rochelle," Tess said.

I reached for the premade spells on the windowsill, then paused, contemplating them for a moment. I would leave them for Tess and Gary.

"You'll remember to use these?"

"Yes," Tess said, speaking through the tears pouring down her cheeks. "Yes, yes. But you aren't going out there, Rochelle."

"I am." I headed out of the room, toward the front entranceway.

Tess moved alongside me, pleading. "This wasn't what the witches set up... Scarlett said the house wards would hold better than the perimeter wards, because you live here. You and Beau fuel them every day. The elves can't get in here."

Gary loomed behind Tess, silent.

"Exactly," I said, pausing with my hand on the front doorknob. "They need me to step out. So they'll kill Beau to make that happen."

"Beau didn't want you going out, Rochelle," Tess said, still trying to remain somewhat collected and rational. "He'd want you to protect the baby. Wait for the witches, for Jade."

"The witches aren't coming, Tess. Not quickly enough. And Jade isn't coming at all. There's just us. Just me."

Tess touched my shoulder lightly. "Please, my girl."

I turned back to her then. Taking in her silver-and-blond-streaked hair, the dusting of freckles across her nose and cheeks. My adoptive mother. My chosen parent. Doing exactly what she was supposed to do, what I'd secretly hoped she'd do. Protecting me.

I smiled. "I love you. I'll be right back. With Beau."

Tess's face crumpled. "No, no. Gary? Gary, stop her."

Gary settled his arm across his wife's shoulders. "I'd go out for you, Tess. Hell, I'd go out right now if I thought I wasn't just going to be in Rochelle's way."

Tess inhaled with a shudder, then wiped the tears from her face. "All right. All right, then." She balled her hands into fists, then marched back into the front living room, going for the spells.

Gary glanced after his wife, grinning despite himself. Then he touched me lightly on the shoulder. "You get Beau over the threshold. We'll be ready for you. For them."

I nodded, taking in Gary's steadfast determination and allowing it to buoy my own resolve. "I need your knife, please."

He immediately tugged a small Swiss Army knife out of the pocket of his jeans and held it out to me, tiny in the palm of his big hand.

I took it and tucked it away in my back pocket. "I'll be right back."

"I know."

I turned, opening the door before I could think about my hastily cobbled-together plan any further. Before I could start to doubt the wisdom of my next move.

I'd seen what was set to happen after this coming moment. I believed that I was taking the first steps to change the future I'd captured in my sketchbook. That vision was recorded, but not contained. It was still malleable—or so I hoped.

I stepped out of the house. It was cold, but the stars were still peering through swathes of dark cloud overhead. The brick underneath my socked feet was gray. I traversed the three steps to the front path, not bothering to look up. The path was also brick, laid by Beau in the fall. He was planning to plant an edging along either side in the spring. But for now, there was nothing between me and the lawn, between me and the elves standing in my front yard.

The door closed behind me. I heard the lock turning. Good man, Gary. A good chosen father.

I stepped onto the grass, instantly soaking my socks.

I looked up.

The elves had turned to face me. Beau was still lying unconscious between them. The elf on the left still held his glass blade across Beau's neck, against his human skin.

I lifted my face to the dim starlight. To the dark night spreading all around us. There were no trees near the house, no deep shadows in which to hide. But that didn't matter.

Because the vision had already shown me how to vanquish the elves. I just had to read between the smudged lines.

"You shouldn't have come at night."

The elves didn't respond.

I took another step away from the protective magic coating the house behind me. That magic might not have been my own, but I understood how it worked. And I didn't want to risk compromising the protections that stood between the elves and Tess and Gary.

I unzipped my hoodie, pulling it off and exposing my rounded belly. I dropped it to the ground, leaving only my tank top and my dual arm-sleeve tattoos between me and the early-morning chill.

The elves glanced at each other.

My strip show was presumably confusing to them. But if I was going to call on the sorcery embedded in the tattoos, I needed my arms bare.

Though I felt a dark certainty that told me I wouldn't need that magic. It wasn't going to come to that.

I pulled Gary's knife out of my pocket, flipping open its inch-and-a-half-long blade.

The elf on the right snorted. He was still favoring his arm.

They had probably expected me to negotiate. But I wasn't great with words. I wasn't witty or snarky. I wasn't a diplomat. That wasn't my role. Others did that much better than I ever would.

They'd been sent to kidnap an oracle. But they were going to have to contend with a dark sorcerer instead.

I sliced my right forefinger with the tip of Gary's knife. A tiny drop of blood welled, black in the low light.

"Like I said. You shouldn't have come at night."

I pressed the spot of blood to my wedding ring. And as I did, I triggered a connection that had remained intact even when Jade had destroyed its anchor—when she'd made Beau and me our wedding bands. It was a connection that had once been bound within the gold and diamonds that my grandmother, Win, had worn in the form of a brooch. But even with that brooch remade, the power it had once held had somehow remained tied to me. Tied to the blood that ran in my veins.

I probably didn't even need to bloody the wedding ring at all, except that it made a powerful focus for my intention.

For my summoning.

I had thought the connection was broken. I'd thought that Jade remaking the brooch into the rings would have destroyed it. But the vision my mother sent me had shown me what I needed to know. What I needed to do.

A demon ripped through the darkness behind me, tearing through dimensions to answer my call. I could already feel its hot breath on my neck and shoulders.

The elves stumbled back a step, both of them raising their swords.

The demon curled its taloned, scaled fingers around my shoulders, shifting upward on its hind legs until it towered over me. Its red-eyed gaze was trained on the elves.

"Protect Beau," I said.

The demon released me instantly, shifting through the front yard like a dark ghost.

The elf with the broken arm vanished without a sound. The second elf pivoted to defend the first, but found himself slashing at empty air.

The body of the first elf dropped to the ground a few feet away. He was still alive. Barely. The second elf spun and spun, looking for an opponent but seeing nothing.

Then he turned toward me, charging wildly. Hair streaming back from his determined face, he sliced forward with his sword. Trying to decapitate me? Perhaps I'd been wrong about the elves' intentions.

The demon snatched him out of the air, then practically bit his head off with a single chomp.

The elf didn't make a sound.

The demon dropped him at my feet, like an offering. Then it hunkered down to steadily gaze at me with its slitted red eyes, emanating contentment.

The first elf was trying to crawl away.

The demon glanced in that direction, then back at me, opening its toothy maw in a deviously playful replica of a smile.

The first elf gained his feet and started running.

The demon loped after him, its pace steady but not at all rushed.

I stepped over the body of the elf who had tried to attack me, crossing to Beau. I crouched next to him, laying my hand on his chest. He was alive, and taking in long, deep, healing breaths.

The demon returned. But it was dragging two elves behind it, rather than just the one that had fled. The angle of the third elf's head suggested his neck had been snapped.

So Beau had gone up against three of them, killing one elf and maiming two. A fierce, completely stupid, utterly vicious pride flooded through me, taking my breath away.

They'd come here. To my home. With only three elves. They had underestimated us.

And they would do it again.

The demon hunkered down across from me. Its jagged-toothed maw was dripping with a clear, viscous liquid that I assumed was elf blood.

Rochelle.

Its voice sounded in my mind, contented and pleased.

A shiver skittered up my spine.

The demon reached out, gently caressing my face as if it had missed me. *Mine.*

I nodded, acknowledging the connection but not thanking it outright.

The demon's eyes glowed a deep red.

Beau groaned, opening his eyes. "Damn it …" But whether he was cursing me, the situation, or the demon looming over him wasn't clear.

The demon shifted its attention over my shoulder, back toward the second elf it had dropped near the path. Then it deliberately drew my attention to the other two elves sprawled on the grass behind it.

Mine?

"Yes," I said, as mildly as I could suggest such a thing. "Take them with you when you go home."

Home? Now?

"Yes, please. I'll call you when I need you." Again, I swallowed an innate desire to thank the demon for slaughtering sentient beings at my request. But even I couldn't ignore my own use of the word 'when.' Not 'if.' When I next summoned the demon. When I next asked it to kill for me. Again.

And when I asked it to protect my child above all else? Was that the next 'when'? The eventual, destined 'when'?

I shook off that dark thought. Focusing on the present was the best way to unmake the future.

The demon leaned toward me, then inexplicably tapped its chin on the top of my head. I curled my hand around Beau's, and he squeezed me lightly in acknowledgement. A heavy silence settled around us.

Then the demon's shudder-inducing chuckle sounded in my mind, and it shifted into the darkness of the cool early morning. First one elf, then two disappeared. More energy bloomed behind me. I glanced over my shoulder to see that the third elf was gone.

I waited, feeling the warmth of Beau's hand in mine. I slowly became aware of my wet socks and chilled arms. Still, I waited.

Nothing else appeared out of the darkness. The elves and the demon were gone.

For now.

"I thought about loading the bodies into the truck, then taking them to Pearl," I said.

"Fuck, Rochelle." Beau squeezed his eyes shut. "Holy fucking shit. That's ... that's ..."

"You're the one who practically tore one of their heads off."

"That in no way equals you feeding three of them to your pet demon."

I smiled at him.

He squeezed my hand again, then offered me a weary smile back.

Like me, Beau had assumed that Jade had severed my connection to the demon when she destroyed Win's brooch at my request. But he didn't bother chastising me for calling the demon to our rescue. Didn't even question how I'd done it. Because that wasn't how we were together.

"Can you move yet?" I asked, shivering.

"If you help me, yes."

Beau rolled to his side, then pushed himself up onto his knees. I gained my feet, leaning down to put his arm over my shoulder. The ivy tattoo on my right arm lifted up and twined around both our arms.

Beau grunted. But when I steadied myself to take his weight, he wasn't as heavy as I expected. The ivy was somehow helping me to lift him.

By the time we retrieved my hoodie and made it to the path, Beau was practically walking on his own. Shifters healed quickly. Thankfully. Because there was no way our day wasn't just getting started.

A second vision hit me just inside the door. Tess was reaching for me, relief etched across her face. Beau was leaning in the doorway. The night was an endless swath of darkness behind him. Behind us.

The white mist of my oracle magic took my sight without warning, flooding through my body, toes to forehead. Overwhelming everything—sight, sound, taste, and touch. I arched up into the onslaught, desperately trying to let it flow through me. Fighting it would make it worse, and if I fell, Beau would catch me, wounded or not.

The mist instantly resolved into a golden-haired woman standing over a body. Relief flooded through me, as for the briefest of moments, I thought I was finally seeing Jade. I thought this vision was a confirmation that the dowser still walked the earth. But I realized that the woman's hair was a darker blond and longer and curlier than Jade's.

Then she looked up, pinning me with her red-eyed gaze.

She was in full vampire mode, fangs on display and fingers flexed. Ready to rend and tear, to rip her prey's heart from its chest and consume it.

"Jasmine ..." I whispered.

Pearl Godfrey was lying sprawled at the vampire's feet. Unmoving ... unconscious ... her skin almost as gray as her hair ...

Dead?

The vision collapsed into mist, then my sight returned.

I was still standing in the entranceway. Beau was holding one of my arms, and Tess the other.

"Living room," Beau snapped, trying to gently prod me forward.

I resisted moving. "No. No. We ... we have to go."

"You'll need to draw," Tess said, her face tight with concern.

"Go?" Beau echoed. "You're not leaving the property. You're not leaving the house, not until the witches come and fix the wards."

I straightened up, standing under my own power. A cool surety replaced the terror that had been rekindled by the vision. I met Beau's gaze, the green of his shifter magic still overwhelming the dark aquamarine of his eyes.

He straightened, stiffened. His expression blanked from whatever he saw in my look.

"I'm sorry," I said.

He shook his head, ready to deny whatever I was going to say.

"The witches aren't coming. We have to go. We have to save Pearl Godfrey."

"Pearl?" Tess murmured sadly. She'd had tea with the head of the Convocation, twice at our house and once at Jade's bakery. She liked the elder witch.

Beau's expression turned stony, obstinate. "Text your warning. Sketch the vision, then ask Blossom to take it to Pearl."

I laid my hand on his chest. "This is the next step."

Tension twisted through his body. I understood his struggle. He was already hurt, and he was scared. Not just for me. He was scared for the baby.

"Whatever we need to do," I murmured, quoting him. "Whatever it takes. Magic wills me this way."

He closed his eyes, trying to deny his own words.

"Beau …" I whispered, feeling utterly terrible for forcing his decision. "Don't make me go alone."

His eyes flew open. They were back to their normal aquamarine. He pressed his hands to my face briefly. "Never, never. Okay … you need shoes … your bag …"

"I've got it," Tess said, already heading for the main stairs. "I'll double check that Rochelle has an extra sketchbook and two sets of new charcoals."

"I'll make sandwiches," Gary said gruffly. Then he laid a hand on my shoulder, telling me with that simplest of gestures that he loved me.

Before I could reciprocate, he turned and hustled back to the kitchen.

I turned to Beau. "I'm sorry."

"Stop saying that. You know I don't need to hear it." He kissed me tenderly. "But I am going to need food. A lot of food."

"There's beef jerky in your stash drawer." I was a vegetarian, but Beau's shifter metabolism practically demanded meat. I enjoyed buying him treats—mostly jerky and Oreos—and tucking them in a kitchen drawer for him to discover.

He grinned. "Thank you." Then his expression became grim. "Pearl?"

I nodded.

"Day or night?"

"Night. Or early morning." Then I pushed through my natural inclination to constantly question myself, to stop myself from jumping to conclusions about the visions. I made a guess, based on how the magic had arrived and departed so quickly. "Soon. Before the night's done. Based on the speed of the vision ... the tenor of the magic."

"Okay. Okay. Text a warning, just in case the witches are paying attention. And ... I'll get some clothing."

I nodded.

Beau shut the front door behind us, then headed up the stairs. I watched him go, desperately wanting to simply admire the view of his naked backside but knowing it wasn't the time.

"Beau?"

He paused, turning back halfway up.

"It's Jasmine ... I think we might be going up against Jasmine."

Beau nodded curtly, seeming completely unfazed at this revelation. Then he continued upstairs.

I pressed my left hand against the wall, feeling magic stir through the barbed-wire tattoo running the length of my arm. Jasmine was a vampire. Newly made, but—as I understood it—with the blood of the executioner running through her veins. She could walk in the sunlight. She was likely stronger than Beau.

But she wasn't stronger than both of us.

And she certainly wasn't a match for my demon.

I retrieved my hoodie from where it had fallen to the tile floor, bending with some difficulty. I didn't want to call the demon again, but I would if it was necessary. I'd already proven I'd do anything to protect Beau. And I couldn't even fathom the dark depths of what I would do to avoid the future I'd sketched for my child.

I was just the same as my mother before me, I realized suddenly. The way she had run from the future she'd seen for me—the way she'd thwarted the vision of what I would become if my grandmother raised me.

But for my own daughter? I would become the woman rendered in black ink by my mother's steady hand before I was even born. The dark sorcerer with the demon and the whip. I would become her in an instant, if that was what it took.

With Beau beside me, though, I could hope … I had hope … that it wouldn't come to that.

I tugged on my hoodie and removed my wet socks, heading into the kitchen to help Gary pack sandwiches and carrot sticks in a paper bag.

We had the head of the Convocation to rescue and a dark future to thwart. Food was a good idea.

I sketched while Beau drove north through the city at speed, both of us guessing that Pearl's house on the waterfront was our destination. As I captured the vision of Jasmine and the elder witch in my notebook, I caught a glimpse of the wrought-iron gate at the top of Pearl's driveway and was able to confirm that assumption.

Point Grey was still relatively quiet at just after four in the morning, as we illegally parked in a residents-only section on a perpendicular street a block south of Pearl's house.

All my text messages to the elder witch since the elf attack had gone unanswered.

I tucked my sketchbook away in my satchel, peering out the windshield at the dark-swathed peaks of the North Shore mountains over top of the beachfront houses. I rubbed the fingers of my left hand together, feeling the charcoal crusted on my skin. Beau waited beside me with his hand resting loosely on the steering wheel, silent but ready.

I knew that he would start the car and be driving away before I'd even finished asking him to do so.

We could run.

We could flee Vancouver in the hopes of foiling the vision of our daughter's future. On our present course, we might actually have been barreling straight ahead into fulfilling that future, drawing closer to it with every step we took. There was no way to tell. Not until I saw a different future.

But Pearl Godfrey would die if we left.

I didn't believe that magic would have shown me the elder witch's death if I wasn't meant to act on it.

"I'm with you," Beau whispered.

I reached for him, threading my fingers through his. He pressed a kiss to my knuckles, then to my wedding ring.

"Rochelle," he murmured. "Oracle... lover... wife... mother... I'm with you." He didn't ask me if I wanted to run. Or if I wanted to change my mind. The question was implicit.

"I love you."

"I know."

I opened my door, and before my feet hit the sidewalk, Beau was by my side. He closed the door behind me, locking the car and lifting his nose to the sky.

"Magic," he murmured.

"Elf?"

He shook his head. "Can't smell them. Well, I couldn't smell them. Not until …"

"Blood had been spilt."

He nodded.

"Jasmine?" I asked.

"No. Witch magic. I think."

Pearl's wards. I settled the strap of my satchel diagonally across my shoulder and chest. It rested over top of my belly, but it wasn't uncomfortable. Not yet. "Okay. We walk east a block, then cross down to Pearl's."

"That's the angle of the vision?"

"I think so. Based on the position of the house, of the hedge … and the gate."

"And … approaching a different way isn't the better choice?"

He meant trying to foil the vision from our very first steps. I raised my face to the dark, cloudy sky, wondering if it was going to rain. Then I started walking, giving my magic leave to guide me if it wished to. And if not? Well, then Beau was quick on his feet and I was fairly certain I could contain Jasmine. If she didn't get her teeth on me … if I didn't go too far and completely wipe her mind …

Ignoring my own doubts, I focused on the feel of the sidewalk underneath my feet, the crispness of the air, and the hush over the neighborhood.

We turned north at the corner.

A wave of magic slammed into me, actually causing me to stumble. My tattoos rippled, shifting, compensating. The magic dissipated.

I started to jog, picking up speed down the short hill. Beau was by my side. Even with the training he forced on me, I was more of a sprinter than a long-distance runner. And being pregnant didn't help with my endurance or lightness of foot, though my second trimester had been less exhausting so far than the first had been.

"Separate and distract," Beau murmured. Then he pulled ahead of me, ducking behind the cedar hedge that surrounded the front yard across from Pearl's house.

Beau had tried to number the series of scenarios he'd been drilling me on during training, in anticipation of being attacked, or needing to escape, or wanting to hold our ground. But I had outright refused to remember what number went with which scenarios when he started alphabetizing contingencies. 'Separate and distract' was attack scenario 2A ... or maybe it was 2B?

Scenario 1 was always the same. Run. But we'd already decided that running wasn't an option.

I was the distraction. And I could do that job far better than sneaking up behind hedges and decapitating foes.

I kept moving, taking advantage of the lack of traffic on Cornwall as I swerved left and the top peak of Pearl's house came into view.

No traffic at all was unusual. It was a busy road, at any hour. So it was an easy guess that magic was holding it back. But whose magic?

Scarlett was standing at the top of Pearl's driveway. Her vibrant, strawberry-red hair snapped and snaked around her head. The blue of her witch magic glowed in her eyes—and reflected along the edge of the thin sword she held between herself and the seven-foot-tall elf standing in the middle of the road.

I kept running, though doing so made no real sense.

A second elf had fallen a few steps behind the first, but was slowly getting to her feet. A third was lying at the top of Pearl's driveway, just outside the domed wards that encased the property. I could see lighter spots within those wards, slowly weaving themselves back together with darker-tinted magic. It was an easy guess that Pearl's defenses had taken several hits from the elves already.

I ran along the hedge, feeling Beau keeping pace with me on the other side.

Scarlett engaged the elf standing before her. More magic exploded between them as their swords clashed.

The witch was courageous and quick. She was also, even to my inexperienced eyes, woefully outmatched.

The second elf gained her feet, manifesting a milky glass sword seemingly out of nowhere.

Still running, I reached for her. She was shorter and slimmer than the elf pressing Scarlett, but still easily a foot taller than me. My tattoos—the ivy and the barbed wire—flowed out from my arms, latching onto the elf's shoulders and halting her midlunge. She snarled, startled.

The larger elf blocked Scarlett's slash, pinning her sword and backhanding her harshly across the face. The witch flew backward through the wards, tumbling across Pearl's front lawn.

I began reeling the elf I was holding toward me. She fought me every step of the way.

The larger elf peevishly slammed his sword across the boundary magic that now stood between him and his prey, Scarlett. Magic reverberated in response. Then he turned and laid his glittering green gaze on me and the elf I had a firm hold on. Repositioning his sword, he took a step in my direction.

A monstrosity erupted out of the hedge behind me. Orange with black stripes and over seven feet tall, it landed next to the elf I held fast. Reaching with massive hands, Beau in his half-human, half-beast warrior form snapped the elf's neck.

The larger elf snarled, pausing to assess the new players on the scene.

"Tear her head right off, Beau," I said. My tone was dark but steady.

Beau ripped the head off the elf. I retracted my tattoos. The body fell with a hard thud to the pavement.

I stepped forward, clearing my path to the larger elf. My tattoos churned around my hands, loose and ready. Waiting.

"Hey, asshole," I said. "I'm sure this isn't the first you've heard of it, but we don't take too kindly to being invaded around here." I held my hands aloft. "By my count, it's Beau and Rochelle four, elves zero. Let's make that five."

Huh. Apparently, I could be witty and snarky—at least when severely pressed.

The elf snarled, manifesting a second sword so that he held one in each hand.

Beau tossed the head he was still holding, as if he were passing the elf a basketball. Except way harder and faster than you'd ever do with a teammate.

The elf sidestepped the spinning head. It hit the wards covering Pearl's property and exploded into a fine powder.

Scarlett had made it to her feet and was slowly stalking across the lawn toward us.

Beau stepped to my side. By my best guess, the elf was slightly out of reach of my tattoos. We waited for him to make his move toward us, wordlessly knowing that we'd execute the same play, just as we'd practiced in case of extreme need—I hold, Beau decapitates.

Pearl stepped out onto the steps at the front of the house. Her gray hair was held back in a tidy bun, and the blue of her magic was simmering in her eyes. I hadn't realized she'd been standing in the doorway. Magic streamed from the elder witch's raised hands, electric-blue beams that originated from each of her fingers. She appeared to be feeding the protective boundary, reinforcing and repairing it.

"Scarlett," Pearl snapped. "Stand down now. Beau and Rochelle have it under control."

Scarlett ignored her mother. Gaining speed as she hit the driveway, she raised her weapon—a jeweled rapier that looked as though she'd sharpened or strengthened it with her own magic. Jade's mother was a sight to behold. Even with the side of her face swelling from the elf's blow, her expression was one of steely determination. I had always thought she looked exactly like Pearl, just twenty years younger. But in that moment, all I could see was her resemblance to every sketch I'd ever rendered of her daughter.

The elf shifted, angling his body so he could keep tabs on all three of us. But he was still slightly out of my reach. I was going to have to close the distance myself.

"Scarlett!" Pearl shouted, stepping down the stairs and along the front path. "That's enough!"

Scarlett blew through the wards at the top of the driveway.

The elf spun to check the strike she was already executing.

I lunged forward, reaching for the elf with my tattoos—but missing.

And suddenly, he wasn't alone.

Three more elves appeared from out of nowhere—but I didn't know whether magic had brought them in, or whether I'd just been so distracted that I hadn't noticed their approach.

All three ignored everything else as they tried to grab for me all at once. Beau knocked the elf nearest to him to the side with a vicious blow. Then he grabbed the second, the two of them tumbling down to the ground in a tangle of limbs and blades and claws.

The third elf managed to get hands on me, lifting me off my feet as if she were executing a snatch-and-run.

So they knew who I was.

But apparently, they didn't know me well enough.

Not bothering to fight the elf's hold, I slammed the heel of my left hand to the gemstone embedded in her forehead, flooding her mind with my oracle magic.

She screamed, loosening her hold on me. But I didn't let her go. Instead, I twined my ivy tattoo around her pale, delicately scaled neck.

Some sort of magical feedback hit my palm, radiating agony through the bones of my hand, wrist, and arm. My arm went numb. Stifling a scream, I kept in contact with the gemstone, pushing back with my magic viciously. The elf stumbled, falling to her knees, which conveniently set me on my feet.

When all that was left of her eyes was the white of my oracle magic, I let her go. She fell at my feet, but I was already turning back toward the fight.

Beau had badly wounded one of the elves, but was locked in a standoff with his second opponent. He was holding the elf's weapons at bay while they attempted to kick out each other's legs.

I reached out with my tattoos, lassoing the elf around his neck. Then, just as Beau met my gaze over the elf's shoulder and released his hold, I yanked the attacker off his feet.

Beside us in the street, but too far away to help, Scarlett fell.

Pearl stepped through the wards. Blue lightning crackled from her fingers.

"No!" I cried.

Beau tore the head off the elf I was choking. I let the body go, desperately trying to redirect my magic. To grab hold of the larger elf that stood between me and Pearl.

That elf was raising his sword, preparing to decapitate the strawberry-haired witch unconscious at his feet.

A lick of Pearl's magic reached out, looping around Scarlett's waist and yanking her out from under the elf's blow. His sword hit the pavement instead, gouging it.

Pearl tossed Scarlett through the boundary behind her. The ward magic caught the strawberry-haired witch, cushioning her fall and gently lowering her to the grass.

More lightning shot out of Pearl's fingers, striking the towering elf looming before her and the wounded elf beside Beau and me. Both elves jerked and spasmed as if being electrocuted. Then they fell, their white armor smoldering and blackened.

Pearl snarled. "You don't touch what is mine to protect, you ingrates."

I stepped over to check on the status of the elf nearest me as Beau did the same for the one close to him. "Pearl, get back behind the wards."

"It's no matter, Rochelle. It's taken care of." Pearl brushed her hands together.

I pinned her with my gaze. "Get back through the wards. Now."

She frowned.

Beau tore the head off the elf he'd paused to check.

The elf at my feet rolled away from me. Distracted, I looked away from Pearl.

Another elf appeared out of nowhere. As if he'd teleported, like Blackwell could. He was holding the arms of two more elves, but he quickly released his companions, who charged me.

Then, somehow, he stabbed Pearl in the side of her chest in the same motion.

Magic exploded between them, throwing the elf and one of his companions backward. Both of them crashed into Beau, who'd already been stepping forward to engage the newly arrived threat.

Pearl fell without throwing out her hands. Without trying to stop herself from hitting the sidewalk.

Latching on to the elf closest to me with both my tattoos, I blasted him with my oracle magic even as I dragged him after me, moving toward Pearl.

A second elf—the one Pearl had dropped with her magical lightning—grabbed my foot, then attempted to stab me in the stomach.

A figure appeared next to me in a blur of white and gold, picking the elf up off the ground and tossing him against the boundary wards. The elf exploded into fine white powder.

I looked toward my rescuer, expecting to see Beau.

I saw Jasmine instead.

"Hey, oracle," she said, cockily stalking over to the elf I held fast.

"Wait … wait!" I cried, desperately looking around for Beau and not seeing him.

The elf I was holding knifed Jasmine. She deflected the blow, though, taking it in the stomach instead of the heart.

I tightened the barbed wire around his neck, cutting into his finely scaled skin.

Jasmine yanked the blade out of her belly.

Choking and clawing at the tattoos I held him with, the elf fell to his knees even as the knife in Jasmine's hand crumbled into white dust.

The teleporter abruptly appeared next to Pearl. He was still grappling with Beau, but obviously trying to get to the elder witch. To finish her off.

Jasmine darted into the fray.

I cinched the barbed wire tighter and tighter around the elf's neck, reeling in my tattoos until he was only a hand's width away from me. I met his panicked gaze.

Then I tore his head off.

Whatever it took.

Whatever the cost.

I released the tattoos. The elf's body fell to one side.

The teleporter threw Beau off him, tossing him across the street and through the cedar hedge behind me.

This left Jasmine standing over Pearl. She looked up, pinning the elf with a red-eyed gaze, her fangs in full view.

My vision realized.

"Try me, asshole," Jasmine snarled.

I stepped forward, reaching for the elf as he readied a lunge for the vampire. But my tattoos responded sluggishly, so that I managed only to brush the back of his neck. I was too far away.

The elf whirled around, spotting me. Then his gaze flicked over my shoulder as Beau erupted from the hedge, racing across the street behind me.

The elf disappeared, teleporting away.

"Behind the wards," I snapped. "Now!"

Jasmine scooped up Pearl and ran down the driveway.

"The bodies, Beau," I said, utterly weary.

"I got them." His words were mangled by his not-quite-aligned jaw.

Headlights flared from up the street. I grabbed the body nearest me, dragging it to the sidewalk. Beau dashed away, collecting the rest.

We crossed through the wards just before the first car passed us. Thankfully the elves no longer triggered the protective boundary magic as corpses. Then, leaving them decomposing and hidden behind the wards in Pearl's front yard, we went to find out who had survived—and to figure out what the hell we were going to do next.

Jasmine was leaning against the wall next to an open doorway—Pearl's bedroom, based on the magic I could feel emanating from it. The vampire opened her eyes, glancing at me. Then she closed them just as quickly.

Her eyes had been blood red.

"Oracle." Jasmine's hands were clenched into fists, and she was pressing her head back against the wall. "I put Pearl on her bed, but …"

I nodded, though she likely couldn't see me. I assumed that she was leaving unspoken how she was wrestling for control around the wounded witch. "You're hurt yourself."

Jasmine pressed her hand against her stomach, covering a clean slice through the brown suede of her jacket, but she shook her head in swift denial. "I should have been faster. We've been at BC Place most of the night … well, early morning now. Trying to figure out what the elves are up to. And I didn't want to leave Mory with only Liam for backup. Benjamin has to go to ground before the sun rises. But I waited too long. I should have been here."

I didn't respond, mostly because I didn't have an opinion. So I stepped through the door into Pearl's bedroom instead. The room was decorated in soft grays and silks. It was large. Which was good, because it currently contained three other witches—all of them seemingly working to keep Pearl alive.

Scarlett was on her feet, but just barely. She stood next to her mother's bed, chanting softly under her breath, with her hands hovering over Pearl's chest. She looked up at me as I entered the room, pinning me with her blazing blue gaze.

"Beau?" she asked.

"He's okay. Scouting the perimeter."

Scarlett nodded, turning her attention back to her mother.

Pearl didn't look great. But her skin hadn't turned the gray I'd seen in my vision, so that was an improvement on what could have been. I also wasn't entirely certain whether Jasmine would have been standing in the hall if she'd faced the elves without Beau and me.

A younger woman, her brown hair streaked with blue, stood on the opposite side of the bed. Burgundy, Mory's friend. I'd met her at Jade's bridal shower. The junior witch was also chanting softly, even as she laid a series of small flat stones on Pearl. They were mostly concentrated around the wound at her ribs, but also in the palms of her hands, at the tops of her thighs, and on her forehead.

"I should have gone out." Another woman was pacing the length of the curtained windows, wearing a burnt-orange wool dress over leggings. I couldn't remember her name, though I was pretty sure we'd been introduced at least once, at Jade's engagement party.

"Someone had to hold off the traffic, and to be here to hold the wards ... if Pearl and I fell," Scarlett said mildly.

"It was ridiculous for both of you to cross the boundary," the orange-clad witch snapped. "There is no way I can hold the grid on my own if Pearl dies. And the house wards will surely fall."

"I know."

A look of dismay flooded across the irate witch's face. "I'm sorry. I'm sorry. Of course, your mother ... she never could have watched you fall."

"Yes," Scarlett said quietly. "It has been an evening of revelations." Then she looked over to me. "And I suspect there are many more to come. You saw Pearl ... getting hurt? That's why you came?"

I nodded. Not bothering to clarify that I might have actually seen Pearl die. Or that I'd tried to text a warning ahead of time.

Scarlett sighed harshly. "Will you take my place, Olive?"

"Of course." The orange-clad witch hustled to Scarlett's side. "And you should let Burgundy look at your wound."

The witch with the blue-streaked hair looked up in response to her name, swallowing harshly. "I'm sorry ... I ... would have been useless out there."

"Well, you aren't useless here," Scarlett said. "And that matters much more in the regular world. We are simply facing ... extraordinary times."

Burgundy nodded, turning back to a wooden box perched on the side table and sorting through more spells. Healing spells, I presumed.

Scarlett turned to me, her face grim and bloodless. "We value the friendship of the wielder's oracle. For saving the life of our coven leader, but also in guiding us forward in the coming battle."

A cavern of doubt and fear opened up by Scarlett's formality threatened to engulf me. By her having titled me, connecting me to Jade—the wielder of the instruments of assassination.

I had no idea how to answer her.

Beau stepped up behind me, wearing his human visage and clad only in sweatpants. It was exceedingly likely that his T-shirt hadn't survived his shift into half-form. But for once, all eyes in the room didn't lock on to him.

No. They were all looking at me, patiently waiting.

Beau laid his hand on my shoulder. "The wielder's oracle is pleased to offer her friendship to the witches of the Godfrey coven. Your magic was fundamental in keeping our human family safe tonight. Thank you."

Scarlett nodded curtly, but she kept her gaze on me.

I finally found my voice. "Jade?"

"Compromised, but alive at last sighting," Scarlett said without emotion. "Jasmine watched the wielder neutralize her companions before she was commanded to go to Pearl by her master, Kett. Liam saw … the fallen being carried into BC Place, which is now coated in elf magic that we're almost powerless to penetrate. Not even the brownie Blossom can get through to Jade."

"Which is probably also why you haven't seen the dowser," Beau murmured, referencing my lack of visions.

"Almost powerless?" I asked.

"Mory," Jasmine answered from the hall, though she didn't step into the room. "Mory and Liam are mapping the damn stadium with her damn dead turtle."

I reached back and twined the fingers of my left hand through Beau's. Then I met Scarlett Godfrey's fierce gaze. "All right, then. Tell me exactly what you need, and we'll see which way magic thinks we should move."

"We need Jade."

I nodded.

"If we cannot vanquish them, then we need to contain the elves."

Crap. Okay.

"In order to do that, we need the grid to … we need to tie the elves into the witches' grid so that we can identify and track them. Then we need to raise the boundary."

I squeezed Beau's hand. "Whatever it takes," I whispered.

He pressed a kiss to the top of my head. "Whatever it costs."

A smile spread across Scarlett's bloodless face, determined and fierce. "Tell me how to get my girl back and save the city, oh oracle."

And hopefully thwart the future I'd seen for my unborn child in the process. Together it was possible, it had to be possible, to foil the vision I was certain my mother's ghost had somehow held, then released for me to record and undo.

I nodded. Energy shifted between us at my acceptance of Scarlett's requests, settling lightly on my shoulders. A magical binding of sorts? Perhaps.

Then a vision hit me like a sledgehammer to the chest, crashing through my limbs and flooding the room with a soft white glow. A series of images flicked through my mind, and I tried to interpret them on the fly before the magic pulled me under.

"Black paint …" I whispered. "The map room …"

Then the vision mist took me, and I saw no more of the present.

Jasmine

*I*t was never so clear to me why vampires weren't natural heroes as it was in the moment I stood pressing myself against a wall in a house full of wounded, possibly dying witches—instinctively hunting them by heartbeat while trying desperately to ignore my bloodlust.

If I didn't count the tasty sip I'd forcefully taken from the werewolf, Lara, I hadn't fully fed in over three days. Most fledglings needed to feed daily—and usually more than once. But I had the ancient blood of the executioner of the Conclave running through my veins, and had been drinking from him exclusively for over seven months. I could walk in the sun, even in the midst of a crowd of humans without fantasizing about the feel of their hearts slowing... and stuttering... as I drained the last drops of blood from their ...

I was doing it again.

Tracking the witches' heartbeats... along with the oracle and the shifter. Though I knew without a doubt that they were more dangerous—possibly unattainable—prey. Because I was wounded.

Wounded and not healing. Not healing as I should have healed, as I assumed I healed.

But then, I hadn't fed for three days... eleven hours... and—

Energy flooded into the hallway, prickling the side of my face and the exposed skin of my neck and hands.

Magic. The power clung to me. The blood already thrumming through my veins surged at its questing touch.

"Black paint ..." Rochelle whispered. "The map room ..."

Oracle magic.

Motion exploded from within the bedroom where Pearl Godfrey lay—possibly dying. Her heartbeat was faint but steady. The shifter Beau, displaying epic miles of gorgeous medium-brown, well-muscled skin, charged into the hall, carrying the tiny white-haired oracle in his arms. The power flooding through Rochelle's eyes was so bright I had to squint against its onslaught.

Beau headed for the stairs to the main floor and disappeared from sight. But no matter how silently the shifter could move, I could still hear his heart. And the amped-up heartbeat of the oracle.

Scarlett stepped into the hall, laying a soul-piercing look on me. Her scent told me she was bleeding. Magical blood.

I crossed my wrists behind my back, digging my clawed fingers into the flesh of my forearms. It was either that or I would pull the strawberry-blond witch into my arms and—

"I'm going to need you to do something for me, Jasmine. You and Beau, if I can convince him to leave Rochelle."

"Lay it on me, momma." My attempt at being flippant was strangled in my dry throat.

Scarlett's eyes narrowed. "First things first. I've texted Teresa Garrick. If you wish to wait in the northeast bedroom, it has a sturdy lock, installed by my mother's former foster child."

She continued down the hall without waiting for my answer, holding herself stiffly.

Powerful prey.

Wounded.

I squeezed my eyes shut, turning my head away. I could still hear the normally charismatic witch's heartbeat. "Wait for what?"

"Blood," Scarlett said, already heading down the stairs. "Teresa is bringing you some of the blood that Benjamin drinks."

Oh... thank God.

I pushed off the wall, turning toward the open door to the bedroom. I locked my gaze onto the mousy-haired witch bent over the bed on which Pearl lay dying. "Scarlett needs to be healed."

"We know," the witch said sharply.

Olive. Her name was Olive. I knew her from before. Before wanting to slake my growing thirst on her blood, before wondering if she tasted of the oranges she grew. A second, younger witch in the room was Burgundy. A friend of Mory's. Friends were important. Friends weren't prey.

The warriors had fallen. I had watched them fall to Jade. Their vanquishing had looked... effortless for the dowser. Now there were too few of us, scrambling to make sense of the situation. It would be better to die myself than to kill anyone who relied on my protection.

"No," I said, hearing the dangerous edge to my voice despite my best intentions. "Scarlett needs to be healed. Now."

Both witches flinched, terror causing their blood to pump faster.

Burgundy and Olive, I reminded myself. Not prey. Burgundy and Olive. "I'll be in the northeast bedroom."

"I'll go to Scarlett," Burgundy said, swallowing her fear of me. Her steadiness allowed me to turn away. "I'll bring ... I'll bring Teresa to you when she arrives."

"No. I ... please don't. Just the ... package." The last thing I needed was a necromancer seeing me in a weakened state. Fighting my instincts was already too difficult, surrounded by those that my blood, my strength, my need deemed as prey. A necromancer of power was not something I wanted to be confronted with. I wasn't certain how I would react. "Thank you."

I made it down the hall and along the short corridor that bisected the house, east to west. Locking myself into a bedroom that appeared to have been recently redecorated in delicate shades of green, I crossed to the window, gazing out into the dark of the early morning. The city of Vancouver was spread out across the bay to the east. And there, just on the other side of False Creek, I should have been able to feel my master, Kettil, the executioner and elder of the Conclave.

Instead, there was just this terrible, aching emptiness. A space Kett had filled, and I hadn't even known it. As if a part of my remaining soul—the part he could communicate with even in the absence of words, the part he commanded—had actually been his.

I thought ... I thought the empty space might mean that Kett was dead. And I didn't know what I was going to do if Jade had ended his immortal existence. If it turned out that he'd allowed the dowser to get close enough to do so, because some long-dead part of him loved her more than his own life.

I would try to kill her, most likely.

Just as she had murdered the part of me that belonged to Kett. The part—the 'me'—that existed because of him. Because he'd taken a chance and brought me back from the oblivion of death. The part, before I'd lost it, that had still dreamed and cared and desperately wanted to survive.

I would die, of course. Squandering the sacrifice of blood and power that Kett had given to remake me. Because Jade had taken out a guardian dragon, her uber-powerful fiancé, and an enforcer werewolf possessed of magical cuffs of strength—and had done so without even hesitating. Without stumbling.

So, too, she must have taken Kett, leaving this black, empty pit of despair lodged within me.

I was no match for the dowser, not even on her worst day. I knew that was true, because I was pretty sure I'd just witnessed Jade Godfrey's worst day ever. So clearly, I would be even less of a match for the dowser on her best day. She would kill me with a flick of her pretty jade knife, then eat a cupcake in celebration. Assuming that the Jade I'd watched trounce all her loved ones still cared about pretty trinkets and tasty treats. I had a feeling she didn't.

And that was another major problem waiting to explode all over the city. Because what else was the dowser using to hold the darkness at bay? What would she do if she awoke from whatever the elves had done to her and found that she'd slaughtered the people she loved?

I had only Liam's accounting of the warriors being carried into the heavily warded stadium. And the sorcerer had indicated that only Jade had still been on her feet, with the guardian of North America slung over her shoulders.

Liam had also said that there'd been a moment when the dowser could have exposed him, could have set the elves on him—but she hadn't.

I pressed my hand against the dark window. My skin was pale, webbed with blue veins. I could see the bones of my wrist and forearm, as if I'd suddenly lost weight.

I dropped my hand, turning away from the darkness.

If Kett was indeed truly dead, I would try to avenge my master. And if it was Jade I'd be facing, then I would die before I landed the first blow.

Vampire instincts were a bitch.

I felt Teresa Garrick the moment she crossed through Pearl's outer wards. And the closer she got—walking the front path, knocking at the front door, stepping inside the house and its extra layer of protection—the more intense the feeling got. I'd never met the necromancer as a vampire. Only once at her home in Seattle, while I'd still been a witch.

Teresa's family had been renowned vampire hunters—before they were all slaughtered, forcing her into hiding. But I'd caught a glimpse of her magic on the witches' grid and had sought her out two evenings before—after Jade had inadvertently informed me that she'd moved to the city with her son, Benjamin, after he'd been remade.

Then I had run away when the necromancer sensed my presence.

Teresa's magic felt nothing like Mory's. The junior necromancer was a welcoming, bright spot. While Teresa was…oblivion walking. Her son, Benjamin, wore a bone bracelet around his wrist to help hold his vampire nature in check. Something like the way Kett's ancient blood helped me maintain control. It was a device of ongoing, working, active necromancy, and it seethed death and domination.

Being near the necromancer herself was even more intense.

I wasn't surprised that Kett's grandsire, Ve, had slaughtered necromancers, snuffing out generations of bloodlines. Or at least that was the tale recounted in almost all the ancient chronicles I'd read about my great-grandsire. We had yet to meet. Kett was wary of bringing me to London, though he'd never voiced his concerns out loud and I'd never pressed him. Ve—again, according to stories—had acquired an immunity to the power that necromancers wielded over death. And Wisteria had whispered tales of Kett himself standing against Teresa, playing with her in a graveyard in Seattle after she'd almost managed to tear him apart with dozens and dozens of zombies.

The entirety of Pearl's house stood between Teresa Garrick and me, and I could tell without question that Kett's immunity had not been passed on to me. Teresa would be able to reach out, take control of whatever remained of my soul, and enslave me.

But no one—no witch or necromancer—would ever own my soul. Not ever again. Which meant that I would slaughter Benjamin's mother before I let her take me. And then I would die.

Why were all the avenues opening before me pointing to death? Had Wisteria truly foiled fate when she'd convinced Kett to remake me? Maybe I was being dogged by destiny.

I felt Teresa's magic abate as she turned around at the front door, crossing swiftly back through the wards and out onto the street.

Unclenching my fists, I became aware that I had retreated through the bedroom and was currently huddled in the deep bathtub of its en suite.

Damn it. I hated it when I moved before I'd even made the decision to do so.

A knock sounded at the door, then footsteps quickly retreated down the hall. Burgundy.

I took a breath I didn't actually need.

I was terrifying everyone, including myself.

After climbing out of the tub, I crossed out of the bathroom, through the bedroom, and to the door. I paused, making sure there wasn't anyone with a heartbeat anywhere near me. Then I unlocked the door and retrieved the box that the young witch had dropped off.

I closed and locked the door, opening the top flaps of the box. Six IV bags of blood were carefully tucked into cardboard sleeves meant to hold wine bottles.

I pressed myself back against the door, nearly weeping at the sight.

I tore the plastic of the first bag too much, spilling blood across my chin. It dripped down my neck as I hastily retreated to the bathroom, pleased to discover that the towels were dark charcoal. No self-respecting vampire wasted blood, not even a drop.

The blood was cold. Even colder than Kett's. And it tasted … flat … thin. Weak. Devoid of Kett's potent, sweet-and-spicy magic, I realized. Other than the sip from Lara—rich, almost blisteringly hot, bittersweet—I had never drunk from anyone other than my master. Kett had sneered at my repeated requests to learn to fend for myself. To hunt and sip. My master had decided that nothing could match the strength he gave me every time I curled up in his lap and latched onto his wrist.

And, as always, he was right. Hell, it had taken me weeks to be able to even prick his skin without assistance. No other blood to be found in Vancouver was more powerful than my master's—at least no blood that wouldn't kill me at first sip. Kett just hadn't implemented a contingency plan for that moment when he'd decided to kneel before Jade's sword, surrendering himself. Possibly surrendering both of us.

I had drained three bags and was working on a fourth before I started to feel steadier. Slowly suckling from that fourth dose, I checked the stab wound in my lower rib cage in the bathroom mirror. It had healed, scarring over. But beneath it, I still felt like part of me was missing. As if the healed skin was only hiding the still-festering wound beneath.

I eyed the last two bags of blood, slightly embarrassed at how much I'd consumed. Which was ridiculous. I had no idea what a normal consumption level was—I usually drank from Kett until I grew sleepy. And second, no one cared. No one was going to be checking up on me. The witches were just interested in keeping me from slaughtering anyone.

A heartbeat moved steadily down the hall toward me—strong and slow, steady, rock solid, powerful. Beau.

He paused outside the door.

I tucked the box and the last of the blood in the empty cupboard underneath the sink.

Beau knocked.

I crossed into the bedroom, unlocking the door and stepping farther back than I needed to open it. Giving the shapeshifter space. I kept my gaze on his left cheekbone. Beau was a tiger, not a wolf with its pack instincts. But he would still instinctively want to exert his dominance over me—the predator in a house full of prey that he protected.

I wasn't stupid, though. I had seen Rochelle behead an elf with her tattoos. I had no idea what kind of magic that was, or how an oracle came to wield it, but she definitely wasn't prey. Moreover, she and Beau were mated—truly mated. And the oracle was pregnant.

With that all in mind, I was actually surprised that Beau hadn't already torn Rochelle from the house, dragging her as far from Vancouver and the elves as he could.

"Jasmine." Beau cast his gaze around the tidy room behind me.

"Beau."

"Scarlett would like to see us. In the map room."

I waited. Beau wasn't an errand boy. He had come for me himself for another reason.

Silence stretched between us until I finally met his gaze.

He regarded me steadily. "Kandy says you bit Lara."

Damn it! "Did she text everyone?"

"Apparently."

"I was under the telepathic elf's influence."

"So she said."

"Well, then."

"You will not be biting me."

I clenched my teeth, chewing on a number of retorts—most of which had to do with him being in no position of authority or strength to be giving me orders. "I won't be biting anyone."

He nodded. But he still loomed in the doorway, blocking out all the light from the hallway with his broad shoulders. "When Rochelle decided she wanted to move here, to settle in Vancouver, I spent some time researching all the Adepts who lived here."

"An ever-growing list."

"True, yes. And now including you and Kett. Vampires. And the executioner has a reputation for collecting magic. People, not artifacts."

"By cultivating relationships. Not by draining them of blood."

"It wasn't Kett who concerned me. He places a lot of value on what Rochelle sees."

"Everyone should."

"Yes." His agreement was blunt, pointed.

"I'm not going to try to slaughter your mate, shifter."

Beau leaned toward me, easily six inches taller than me. He inhaled deeply. "I know how to kill you, Jasmine. Vampires aren't immortal."

I clenched my fingers, then unfurled them—instead of slamming my hand against his chest. Instead of proving that even if he knew the methods that would lead to my eventual death, he would find them difficult to pull off.

"Vampires are immortal, actually." I leaned farther into his space, breathing in the heady scent of his warm blood. "Perhaps you've been misinformed."

"It's difficult to survive without a head," he snarled.

I laughed, and the resulting sound was darker than I'd intended. "That depends on how quickly you re-attach it."

Beau reared back—though not in fear. To get a better look at me.

"Am I lying?" I asked mockingly.

Shifters could smell lies—or at least could sense them through an increased heart rate. And of course, I didn't have a heartbeat. Not a regular one, anyway.

He narrowed his eyes. "We're on the same page."

"We are."

He nodded curtly, then turned to walk down the hall.

The shifter was deliberately baiting me, turning his back like I was of no consequence—whether or not he'd intended it. I ignored the urge to spring forward and latch onto his neck.

He was just walking ahead of me down the hall, for goodness' sake. Not everything was about games. Or blood.

I stopped by Pearl's room, staying just long enough to ascertain that Olive and Burgundy had managed to erect a stasis field, through which they could take shifts monitoring minor changes in the wounded witch's health. I couldn't see the casting—even as a witch, I hadn't had any sight for magic. But I could feel a tingle of energy from it. So far, Pearl wasn't dying. But no magic usage came without a cost, and if the elder witch didn't start holding her own in the next forty-eight hours or so—let alone improve—then the witches who were trying to help her heal were going to need to recharge.

What we really needed was a healer. Problem was, the Godfrey coven didn't have one. In fact, since the death of my Aunt Rose, the Convocation didn't even have a healer occupying one of their thirteen seats.

As I left the witches, I began to realize that even flush with human blood, ignoring their heartbeats was impossible. I hadn't appreciated how much Kett had insulated me with his powerful, ancient blood.

Beau was waiting at the base of the main staircase, but he quickly headed toward the basement when he saw me.

I caught up to him, but didn't press too close. For both of our comfort levels. The house was dark, as if no one had bothered turning on any lights when the elves' attack had drawn them from their beds or from the map room. I was pretty sure that Burgundy had been on shift, but I was less certain whether Scarlett had even left to change or shower or sleep since I'd brought the news of Jade being compromised. And Olive was staying with Pearl for the duration of Jade's wedding festivities. I wondered if anyone had thought to cancel the caterers and the florist—

"It's bad, then?" Beau asked in a whisper. "With Pearl?"

"Yeah, it's bad."

Beau said nothing else as we neared the door to the room that held the central hub of the witches' grid. A laundry room, bathroom, mechanical room, and a neatly organized storage room were accessible farther down the hall. I'd been spending as much time in Pearl Godfrey's basement as I was allowed to. The grid map fascinated me. I'd been working on figuring out how to tie its magical detection system into a computer inter-face, so that Kandy could receive alerts automatically or even access the map from her phone. But it had been slow going. It was a monumental task—and would have been so even if my tech magic still came to me as easily as it once had.

The map room occupied what had once been a recreation room that took up at least half of the foot-print of the house. The door stood open.

Pearl's home was modestly sized, at least compared to the real estate the Fairchild coven held. But seeing as how it occupied a chunk of low-bank waterfront in Van-couver, it was an easy guess that it was worth even more than the currently empty and gutted Fairchild estate.

I pushed the thoughts of that house, of that base-ment—the site of my human death—out of mind just by stepping into the converted rec room. A detailed map of Vancouver had been painstakingly painted across all four of its walls. Usually a chair sat in the center of the room, but that had been moved to the hall.

In the room now, Rochelle was slowly painting an intricate design on the tightly woven berber carpet. The white of her oracle magic blazed from her eyes. Including the previously plain-white baseboards, she had covered nearly half the room in twisted vines of ivy and barbed wire. Tucked into the curls and spiked waves were other seemingly random objects...a snake, links of a chain or necklace, a sliver of a crescent moon. And there were more images that I couldn't even guess at...runes maybe...or Elvish script even, depending on what the oracle was channeling.

Scarlett was standing at the center of the room. A basic circle encompassed her bare feet. I had a feeling that Rochelle was working toward tying that inner circle to her intricate design. But in hope of creating what? Making Scarlett function as what? An all-seeing quarterback?

"We need an elf," Scarlett said. Hands on her hips, she was wearing a simple black silk sheath that fell to her calves. Her strawberry-blond hair cascaded across her shoulders and down her back. She no longer reeked of blood, but she still wasn't completely healed. "Jasmine?"

I nodded. "You want to try tying the elf blood to the map? To see if that will help the magic of the grid track them?" I had floated that idea to Jade and Kandy even before I'd first laid eyes on the map room, and the witches and I had discussed it again after I'd brought the news to Pearl that Jade had been compromised. "How much do you think we need?"

Scarlett turned to look at me. "All of it."

Dread flitted through my stomach. It was an emotion I'd had no idea I was still capable of in this new immortal, invulnerable form. "You want... you want me to capture an elf alive?"

"You and Beau."

"Then what? A... sacrifice? You're going to slit a sentient being's throat and bleed him out?"

Scarlett's expression turned grim. "I won't be able to do it. The oracle has indicated that I need to stand in the circle and that nothing can cross into it with me."

I closed my eyes, feeling a little faint. And not because I hadn't drunk enough.

"I can do it," Beau said.

"No." Scarlett's denial was absolute.

"I'm the vampire," I whispered. "Bloodletting is my... deathly deed to deal."

"Yes."

Seven months. That was how long I'd been a vampire. That was how long Kett had shielded me from my true nature.

But Kett was gone. Possibly dead. And many, many others were going to die if the elves had their way. Not that I knew what they were up to, but it had to be seriously nefarious if they'd taken out all the warriors and were now attempting to pick off the witches.

It was time to take off the training wheels.

"All right," I said, thankfully sounding much more detached and focused than I felt. "Where do we find an elf? We should stay away from BC Place, if possible. We don't want to draw attention to Mory and Liam."

"I agree." Scarlett pointed to her left. About a quarter of the way up the wall, a location glowed softly blue, tinted with gold.

"The bakery?"

"The magic keeps flaring," Scarlett said. "I believe the elves are trying to breach the wards."

"Why? Does Jade hold objects of power there?"

Scarlett nodded. "And the portal."

"Excuse me? There's a portal in the bakery? Like … permanently?"

"It's guardian magic. An anchor point, I suppose. But I doubt the elves could tap into it."

Doubt? Doubt? Holy hell. I momentarily lost my mind imagining what the elves could do if they tapped into a power source of that magnitude. And then … then I put two and two together. Or at least I attempted to inject a bit of rational conjecture to my rapidly dissolving day. The sun hadn't even risen yet.

"If they had Jade under control," I said thoughtfully, "and if the elves wanted into the bakery, why wouldn't they just use the dowser? And actually, that would hold for getting through any wards in Vancouver. The dowser practically walks through wards that she isn't even keyed to, doesn't she?"

A brilliant smile spread across Scarlett's face, filled with love and magic. The power of charm and charisma that the witch wielded so effortlessly brushed against me, filling all the empty places that Kett's disappearance and the stab wound had created.

Beau shifted, rolling his shoulders.

Then Scarlett's involuntary magic dissipated. Pressing my hand to the invisible wound at my rib cage, I felt utterly bereft. Possibly even worse than before.

"Yes," the witch whispered, turning her attention to the opposite wall and the black-sketched outline of the stadium, BC Place. It stood out, surrounded in pale-green magic, almost white—the elves' wards. "My girl would never let anyone hold her."

I didn't repeat the fact that Jade had been influenced so heavily that she had taken down a guardian dragon, her fiance, and one of her best friends. I could

speak only to what I'd seen, not whatever had come
after. Or whatever was going on now. That wasn't my
task, it seemed. Because apparently, I wasn't the brains
in the new order running Vancouver. Just the hired gun.

I shook off the sense of heaviness. There was no difference between hunting an elf and capturing them alive,
and killing one to protect myself and others—which I
would do without question. Except there was a difference, of course. But there shouldn't have been. Kett
wouldn't have hesitated to take on the task. Hell, he'd
have done it and been back by now.

"The bakery," I said, glancing at Beau.

He nodded. "I'm with you." He looked toward
Rochelle.

The oracle was crawling backward toward
Scarlett, connecting the inner circle to the outer design
as I'd thought she might. Still in the grip of her magic,
Rochelle hadn't acknowledged our presence at all.

"She'll need water," Beau said. "And apples, if you
have any."

Scarlett nodded. "Burgundy will care for Rochelle.
If she finishes the spell before you return."

"Well, then. Let's go hunt an elf," I said overly
brightly. "How hard can it be to keep one alive?"

Beau grunted, amused. "I suggest an ambush and a
concrete brick to the back of the head."

"Seems reasonable."

As it turned out, ambushing the elf would have been a lot
easier if he hadn't already held the higher ground. Well,
not higher, exactly. But definitely exposed. And soon to
be even more out in the open as the sun rose. Dawn
came late this time of year, but over half the apartments

were already lit to either side of the alley behind Jade's bakery. Thankfully, most people still had their curtains drawn.

The elf in question was pacing before the exterior steel back door, moving back and forth between the bakery's green recycling bin and a black garbage bin midway between the door and the neighboring wine store.

I paused at the mouth of the alley on Vine Street, a half block north from West Fourth Avenue. Though we could have easily walked to the bakery from Pearl's, given that our intent was to kidnap an elf, Beau and I had borrowed Pearl's car, parking it at the corner of Vine and West Third. Close enough to get to it quickly, but far enough away that we could still sneak up on the elf.

The occasional car drove past, but I was tucked against the side hedge and fence of a converted house on the corner, and the elf didn't notice me. Without any discussion, Beau had crossed up toward the corner when we'd first spotted the intruder, his footsteps silent on the grass that edged the paved sidewalk. Hands shoved deep into the pockets of his hoodie and head bowed, he would scout forward of my position, double-checking for any elves at the front of the bakery.

The elf had outfitted himself in what appeared to be purloined sports gear printed with a soccer team's logo. He glanced both ways up the alley, just after Beau had stepped out of sight. He then peered up at the sky. It was an easy guess that he was concerned about exposure and the rising sun as well.

And, just to complicate the situation further, I wasn't certain whether or not Gabby was already inside baking. I'd gotten her number from Mory—keeping Liam out of the loop so we didn't risk him running in with guns blazing—and texted her before we left Pearl's. I hadn't gotten an answer yet, though only about seven minutes had passed.

If Gabby had shown up for her shift while the elf was trying to break in, I wasn't sure whether he would have tried to use the junior amplifier to gain entry. Jade's wards didn't work like that—only the dowser could grant safe passage through them. But whether the elf would have tried anyway, I had no way of knowing. Alternatively, the warrior—currently covering his armor with a brand-spanking-new sweatshirt and sweatpants—might have allowed the amplifier to enter the bakery, using her to study the wards.

I pulled my phone out of my jacket pocket, sending a second text message to Gabby, just in case.

Stay inside the bakery.

The elf stepped back up to the exterior door, holding his hand forward as if feeling the energy that encased the building. Then he started moving his hand, almost as if he were drawing in the air. He slowly boxed out the entire door with his gestures. Then he reached for the door handle, actually managing to grasp it before staggering back and shaking his hand as if he'd been burned.

If I'd been capable of seeing elf magic, I would have been able to view exactly what he'd been drawing. But either way, it was a safe bet that he was a ward breaker of some sort. Like a code breaker or a hacker, but with magic. He was either trying to sever or neutralize Jade's wards, but limiting the scope to the perimeter of the door. Smart.

Beau appeared behind me, arriving from the opposite direction.

I glanced at him.

He shook his head.

No other elves, then. Or none that Beau could sense, at least—but that was actually a problem, since none of us seemed capable of sensing the elves before they chose to reveal themselves. So there might have been a half-dozen of them hiding in the ever-lightening shadows at the edges of the alley.

Except... the illusionist was dead. I had seen her sprawled on the ground. I'd seen Jade with the illusionist's gemstone drilled into her forehead.

So maybe it was just the one elf—leaving us to hope he couldn't also teleport. But the little information I'd cobbled together about the elves made it fairly clear that they specialized as Adepts did. Warriors, illusionist, telepath, teleporter. The ward breaker in the alley might have channeled magic similar to that of an Adept sorcerer—and it was likely the only magic he channeled.

"Can't sneak up on him," Beau whispered, practically pressing his lips to my ear as he articulated the concern that already had me hesitating. "And he's thinking of leaving."

I nodded, whispering back, "His magic is different than the others. Though that doesn't mean he can't do the knife trick."

"They all seem to be able to do that."

"But if you hear him muttering or see him drawing anything... well, try to stop him before he finishes."

Beau nodded. "And our approach?"

"If you can't be sneaky, be brash." I reached up, unbuttoning my suede jacket and then the top buttons of the silk blouse I was wearing underneath. With my cleavage on display, I fluffed my hair, fanning it over my shoulders.

Beau snorted. "Here's hoping he likes vampires. And females, for that matter."

"He'll at least look. All I need is eye contact." That last claim was a bluff. I had never actually tried to beguile anyone except Kett. And he hadn't even noticed my futile attempts.

I sauntered into the alley, swaying my hips a little more than I needed to in order to walk.

The elf immediately locked his gaze on me. A short blade appeared in his hand, but he kept it pressed against his leg.

I allowed an enticing smile to curl my lips. I might not have been a warrior by the high standards of the Adepts who called Vancouver home, but I was a vampire. And vampires seduced their prey.

At least as far as I'd figured things out so far.

I slowly prowled toward the elf, moving languidly. Playing at being a little drunk. I caught a curl of my hair, smoothing it through my fingers and holding the gaze of the bigger predator in the alley.

I was supposed to be able to ensnare, to beguile. Though even if I actually wielded such magic, whether it would work on an elf, I had no idea.

Ten steps away, though, the elf still hadn't raised his weapon.

"Hello," I tittered. "Are you looking for Jade?"

The elf stiffened, but he didn't glance away from me.

"Sometimes," I whispered secretively, "she'll share cupcakes before the bakery opens." If not for the worry over whether Gabby was there, I might have been able to drag the elf through the powerful wards that coated the building. Except since the elf wasn't keyed to that magic, I'd be hoping that trying to do so wouldn't fry me along with him.

"I'm not interested in cupcakes," the elf spat. His English accent was thick, but I couldn't attach any specific place of origin to it.

I allowed my smile to widen, then touched my tongue to my teeth. "Oh yes? What does interest you?"

He looked confused by the question. Maybe even a little glassy-eyed. So had I actually managed to beguile him? How was I supposed to know?

The elf smiled, displaying sharp-pointed teeth. The effect sent a shudder up my spine.

But instead of fleeing, I leaned into him, gently placing my hand on his shoulder. He was over a foot taller than me.

He grabbed my shoulders, pressing me back against the building. The motion was hard, perhaps even bruising. Except I didn't bruise easily.

"What are you doing?" he snarled.

I laughed teasingly, toying with the string ties of his sweatshirt. "Don't you like to play?"

"Play?" He frowned.

I reached up, keeping his gaze locked with mine as I stroked his jaw, trailing my fingers down his neck. "Yes ... play."

His expression softened.

Beau was slipping along the edge of the fence toward us, trying to keep to the shadows. Except the sky was brightening to the point where doing so was about to become difficult.

I ran my tongue along my teeth again, realizing that my canines had sharpened. Lengthened.

The elf watched my every move, enraptured.

I smoothed my hands over his shoulders, readying to grab him before Beau struck.

The elf suddenly grimaced, pressing his hand to the gemstone in his forehead.

I felt my hold on him slip—a hold I hadn't been entirely certain I'd actually established.

Then Gabby threw open the exterior door, carrying a light-green composting bag.

The elf's gaze snapped to her.

Ah, hell.

Instinct kicked in. I surged forward, lifting up onto my tiptoes and sinking my teeth into his neck.

The elf snarled, slamming me back against the building even harder this time. I hung on. His thick blood instantly coated my face and lips, pouring down my throat though I wasn't trying to drink. He slammed me back again and again, but I clamped down even harder, desperately hoping my venom subdued him before he cracked my spine.

Gabby cried out. Her delayed reaction time gave me a hint of how quickly the elf and I were moving, grappling.

Beau grabbed the amplifier, shoving her back through the wards into the bakery kitchen.

The elf stabbed me.

Two short blades embedded into either side of my ribs, slicing through my flesh, then getting caught on bone. Pain flooded through my torso, radiating up into my chest. The elf twisted the blades, presumably trying to free them—but feeling more like he was destroying the very magic that held me together. Carving me out from the inside.

I tore at the flesh of his neck, desperately trying to keep ahold of him. He stumbled, slowing. Perhaps my venom was starting to affect him. But he still managed to withdraw his blades. They felt even worse exiting than they had in the stabbing.

He was going to knife me again.

I wasn't certain I would survive a second attack.

Beau appeared behind the elf, walloping him over the head with a heavy-bottomed cooking pot. The blow reverberated through my teeth, which were still latched to his throat, then into my head.

I released my prey, stumbling back against the building.

The elf whirled to answer Beau's blow, belatedly raising knives that were sticky with my blood. He was moving as if drugged.

Beau flipped the pot, deftly slamming it up underneath the elf's chin.

The elf's head snapped back. He dropped to the ground between us.

The intense magic of Jade's bakery wards churned on the exterior wall behind me. I pressed my hands against it, holding myself upright. The elf at my feet took a ragged breath.

I looked up. Beau stood on the other side of my prey, facing off with me. And for a moment, I considered lunging over the elf and taking out the loss of my prize on Beau's throat. I could already feel the heat, could taste the spice of his sure-to-be-thick-and-sweet blood flowing down my throat.

"Do we have a problem?" Beau asked. His voice was edged with the growl of his beast.

I didn't want to face off against the massively strong shifter I'd seen in action only a couple of hours before. But I was, unfortunately, experiencing another completely instinct-fueled, utterly irrational moment.

I squeezed my eyes shut. Not prey, not prey.

"I repeat. Do we have a problem?"

"No problem, pretty kitty." I had intended the comment to be playful, but my words dripped with a dark and unsteady resolve. Then I bent over and vomited up elf blood. It splattered across the pavement and the toes of my boots. And even as I waited to see if I was going to throw up a second time, I watched as the regurgitated blood solidified, turned into a fine crystal, and was partially blown away by a gust of wind.

Ah, hell. Jade had warned me not to bite the elves. She'd been joking, but I certainly didn't like the idea of the blood thickening or crumbling into crystal inside me.

"Jasmine?" Gabby asked.

Still bent over, I swiveled my head to take in the amplifier. The lithe blond was standing by the open back door, still within the protective wards. She was wearing a ruffled pink apron and holding a copper pot. She also had a cordless earbud in one ear.

"Are you? Are you … your eyes are … red."

"Next time, check your text messages," I snarled.

Gabby took a hesitant step back, babbling. "I'm sorry. I'm so sorry. Sometimes I listen to music while baking … and I … text messages interrupt … so—"

Beau raised his hand, silencing the fledgling.

She clamped her mouth shut.

I squeezed my eyes shut a second time, straightening as I attempted to get myself under control. I pressed my hands over the stab wounds on either side of my ribs. They had closed, but it hurt to touch them. As if maybe some of my magic, the magic that held me together, had been destroyed.

"How hurt are you?" Beau asked. "I can carry both you and the elf … but it might draw too much attention."

I nodded, pushing past the grip of the pain radiating through my chest—and my almost overwhelming need to appease that ache with Beau's blood … and now

Gabby's. "We'll carry him between us. Like he drank too much and we're just getting him home."

"Right." Beau hunkered down to pick up the elf.

I twisted my hands together behind my back. It was either that or latch them around his neck. "Go back inside, Gabby," I said. My voice was steady and sure. Thank God. "We're okay."

Beau got the elf upright, his head lolling to one side, then the other. I transferred my grip to the elf's left arm, getting it over my shoulder, then holding on. Not for my life, but for Beau's. Though as wounded as I was, I had no idea whether I could take down the werecat. Not when my behavior was probably already triggering every predator's instinct he had.

Gabby was still gripping the pot like she might actually use it as a weapon. To me, she looked like frightened but fierce prey as she stepped back onto the tile floor of the kitchen. Then she watched us leave from the open doorway.

"Everything is so screwed," I whispered. "Upside down, wrong way around."

Beau grunted in agreement. Then we stuffed the elf in the back of Pearl's car. We made sure he'd stay unconscious and be able to accompany us through Pearl's wards with a premade spell Scarlett had prepared, which Beau clipped to his sweatshirt. Then we took him to slaughter.

Beau drove us back, parked the car in Pearl's below-ground garage, and single-handedly dragged the still-unconscious elf from the back seat—all without saying anything about me having spent the trip gripping one side of my seat and the door handle so hard that I left both permanently dented.

Biting the elf had been a bad idea. Inadvertently drinking his blood had been even worse. But getting knifed by his crystal blades? I felt as though my inner core, everything that was holding me together, had been sliced so deeply that it would never heal, never become whole again.

I had to move. I had to get out of the car. On my own.

I still had to help Scarlett bind the elf magic to the grid. Otherwise, the witches—the last of the city's defenders—were completely blind. I might have been dying, but if I didn't get out of the damn car, everyone else would be joining me.

Burgundy was waiting at the open door to the basement, leaning down to clip another premade spell to the elf's sweatshirt before Beau carried him in. The first spell was what had allowed us to drive the elf through the property wards, but the house wards presumably needed their own override. With Pearl out of commission, those wards would normally allow entry only to those she'd already invited.

A terrible pain tore through my midsection. I clenched my teeth, suppressing my need to scream. I pressed my hands to my belly, to my rib cage, convinced that I'd actually been ripped in half. I hadn't been, though. No gaping, seething wounds.

I blinked away tears of pain, hoping to God that they weren't composed of blood. Hoping that vampires crying blood was just another urban myth. I knew that my remade body produced other fluids—or saliva, at least, because I would have noticed my teeth being stained red all the time.

Beau dragged the elf into the house. But Burgundy stayed waiting for me at the door. It wasn't the time to be contemplating whether or not I could produce spit...or snot...or anything else without it being composed of blood.

If I sat in the car for too long, Beau would come back and try to carry me. And touching me would have been a really, really bad idea.

If I were triggered, I might try to slaughter every warm-blooded person in the house. Slaughter the very Adepts I was trying to become friends with...to build a life around ...

I felt like sobbing. Then raging. Then curling up on the floor of the car and simply willing myself to die.

I did none of those things. I opened the car door and walked into the house. I managed to nod at the junior witch waiting for me. I might have even smiled.

"Are you all right?" Burgundy asked.

"Still moving."

She nodded, twisting her hands together. Her magic dimly outlined her fingers. I blinked and the blue aura ghosting her hands disappeared. Had I actually seen her magic? That was an odd side effect of dying.

I forced my attention onto more important things. "And Pearl?"

Burgundy looked grim. "No change. We could use...another witch."

Scarlett, she meant. Except Scarlett was a little busy trying to protect an entire city from invading elves.

Burgundy glanced to her left. Halfway down the hall, Beau had dumped the elf's body by the door to the map room, then stepped inside. I could hear his heartbeat, along with two others.

"I...I'd better get back," Burgundy said. "I just wanted to make sure you were both okay. And that you could get the elf through the wards."

"Thank you."

Burgundy nodded, hustling off toward the stairs to the main floor. I managed to not lunge after her and tear her beating heart out of her chest. But it felt like a near thing.

I made it down the hall, pressing my back to the wall a couple of feet away from the elf. I could hear the murmur of conversation emanating from within the map room—Beau and Scarlett—but I wasn't paying attention to their actual words.

I just had to get through this next part. Then I could retreat, lock myself in the upstairs bedroom, and drink the last two bags of blood.

That wasn't going to be enough, of course. I was fairly certain I was dying. But hopefully, with the human blood to hold me, I'd lapse into a coma first and not take anyone else with me.

Beau stepped out from the map room. He was carrying Rochelle, but she was awake. He nudged the elf with his foot, checking for signs of consciousness.

"Closer, Beau," the oracle murmured.

Protective instincts slammed energy into my limbs, and I pushed off from the wall. Even in my present state, I wasn't going to let the oracle go anywhere near a wounded elf.

But it was me she'd meant. Me that she was reaching for with fingers covered in dried black paint. The white of her magic simmered in her eyes.

I knew what might happen if I let anyone touch me. And I stepped forward anyway, so that Rochelle could brush her slim, warm fingers across my cheekbones.

"Jasmine," she murmured. "It's going to be okay."

Damn it. I was the one who should have been consoling and guiding her...and Beau, and Burgundy. There were only three witches in this house who were older than me. And one of them was unconscious, one of them didn't have the magic to lead—and one of them was waiting for me to step up.

"Of course," I said. Lying.

"See?" Rochelle said. "I see you ..."

Her magic reached out and bit into my mind, offering me the briefest glimpse of a golden-haired, creamy-skinned woman on a wet cobblestone street. The woman was surrounded by buildings whose look reminded me somehow of Europe. And she was...me. Me as a vampire. The shock of recognizing myself was visceral. An energizing jolt to my system.

In the vision, the vampire glanced over her shoulder and smiled. Coy, playful...and fully in command of herself. Me. Myself.

Alive. And in London, at best guess.

So I was going to survive. The vision wasn't delivered with a timeline, of course, so I could still lapse into a coma first. But...I wasn't going to die. Or I wasn't meant to die. Not yet anyway.

My sight cleared, and the long, dark hallway came back into focus. Beau had already turned toward the stairs with Rochelle protectively bundled in his arms. Thankfully, being touched by the vision had somehow given me a reprieve from wanting to stalk after the pair and tear out their throats. Which would have been an act of idiocy, really. A complete waste of powerful blood.

I was going to make it through. Alive. In some fashion, at least. If I believed that the future couldn't be altered.

I stepped around and over the elf, standing in the doorway to the map room. The intricate web of vines, barbed wire, and symbols, all drawn in still-drying black paint, now connected all four walls to the simple circle in the dead center of the room.

Scarlett, still barefoot in her simple black sheath, sat cross-legged in the middle of the circle. She opened her eyes, pinning me with the electric-blue magic blazing from them. Magic I shouldn't have been able to see so clearly. And it was joined by a power rising from the floor that I really shouldn't have been able to feel so intensely.

I squared my shoulders. "Where am I to stand?"

"In each of the corners."

That was the nice way of saying I needed to bleed the elf four times. "I assume I should avoid stepping on the design?"

Scarlett smiled, her expression serene—but with an edge that had been growing sharper since Pearl had fallen. "You assume correctly."

I cleared my throat. "Is there a…knife I'm supposed to use? Blood sacrifices usually call for such things, don't they?"

"You are the blade today."

I nodded, stepping back to the elf and bending down to lift him across my shoulders before I could run away screaming like a coward.

I was a goddamn vampire. In the most literal sense of that phrase, if some of the lore was to be believed.

The elf was heavy, but I had yet to find something I couldn't actually lift at least a couple of inches. Kett frowned at such banal tests of power, so I had to conduct my feats of strength on the sly. And since the executioner rarely left me alone, I actually had very little idea of what I was capable of doing.

But I could help the witches try to save Vancouver from the elves. Someone had to do the dirty deeds. And today, that person was me. Me and Scarlett. And if a witch who was best known for her charm and charisma could step up, then so could I.

I moved into the room, carefully picking my way over to the easternmost corner—at least as best as I could judge direction by the feel of the rising sun beyond the concrete and earth that surrounded us. A triangle of vines on the floor there left just enough space for me to set the elf on his knees and hold his back against my hips and torso. I could feel blood pumping through his throat underneath my fingers. The wound I'd opened with my teeth in the alley had completely healed.

"Jasmine ..." Scarlett whispered.

I looked up from contemplating the creature—the sentient being—I was about to murder in cold blood.

Scarlett smiled, but she was crying. Tears slowly slipped down her alabaster cheeks.

"For my master," I said. "For Kandy, and Warner, and ... Jade. To protect everyone that the elves are planning on murdering."

"Yes."

I gouged the elf's throat open with my sharp fingernails, just enough that thick white blood spurted, then sprayed across the entire corner of the room. The wound in his neck closed almost immediately.

The magical design painted in black across the carpet seemed to writhe. Then somehow, it absorbed the elf's blood before it could solidify. The vines and barbed wire between me and the edge of Scarlett's circle glowed the white of the oracle's magic, then faded.

"Again," Scarlet murmured.

I picked up the elf, moving clockwise. As if I were still a witch, and not a vampire executioner.

I ripped open the elf's throat again. The runes and symbols lapped the blood up once more. But this time, the white glow didn't entirely fade.

I moved on to the third corner, repeating the process. And as I did, I began to feel the elf dying.

Three-quarters of the room was glowing. I stumbled as I crossed to the fourth and final corner, briefly worrying that I'd taken a wrong step and possibly contaminated the intricate spell. But either the paint was dry, or it wasn't thirsty for my magic.

I bled the elf dry in the fourth corner. I slit his throat with my sharp fingernails over and over, until the wound on his neck no longer closed. I felt him die. Then, utterly exhausted, I sat with him draped across my lap, watching as he began to decompose, crumbling into a fine powder from the inside out.

I wept.

Possibly for my mortal soul.

Glowing so brightly white that I had to squint to see past it, the potent, well-fed magic etched across the baseboards and the carpet shifted and stirred. It began to slither and slide, snaking backward from each corner and feeding into the simple circle in which Scarlett stood.

Somehow, every speck of paint, every bit of the design Rochelle had worked across the floor, went with the magic as it moved. And in the end, the only thing in the room other than the map on the walls, me, and the elf decomposing in my lap was a witch in a circle of pure white energy.

"Go now, Jasmine," Scarlett said, her voice heavy with magic. "Leave the elf's body. It will continue to feed the spell. But … I need you to step out of the room."

I tried to obey her, shifting the elf off my legs. But I wasn't able to stand. So I crawled. Moving toward the door so, so slowly. I wasn't certain I was going to get out of the room before whatever Scarlett was doing, whatever power was building, consumed me as well.

Two sets of firm hands grabbed my shoulders and arms, dragging me through the doorway and into the hall. I managed to get to my feet even as intense magic erupted behind me, slamming the door shut and throwing me to the hall floor.

I rolled over. Beau stood over me, his eyes glowing green.

"Thank you ..." I tried to kneel.

Then I saw the black hole standing beside Beau. The deep hole of oblivion that had come for my immortal soul.

Teresa Garrick.

The necromancer had returned.

I screamed. God help me, I screamed. I couldn't be owned. I couldn't be controlled by anyone else. Not ever again.

"Enough, vampire," Teresa snapped. But more peeved than angry.

"Please ... please ..." I wept, desperately trying to crawl down the hall toward the stairs. "Please. I'd rather be dead."

"Amusing." Teresa's sneering laugh crawled up my spine. "Since you already are."

She reached for me.

I blacked out.

I hadn't really slept since I'd first woken as a vampire. I had felt the tug of the sunrise from time to time, and often curled up in the luxurious linens Kett favored—even though he never used the bed. I dozed after feeding. But I never slept.

So when I woke this time, supine on a bed with my hands carefully folded across my rib cage, I thought I was ... before. Before my remaking. As the white-painted, coffered ceiling came into focus, I found myself thinking that maybe I was Jasmine Fairchild again. Tech witch. Sister to Declan, cousin to Wisteria. Maybe ... maybe I was Betty-Lou, and we three lived together, protected from the world, from our family, behind a white picket fence we'd built together. Betty-Lou. Betty-Sue. Bubba.

Then the hunger hit.

It ripped through my body. It flung me off the bed. Without thinking—because there was no place in me for thought anymore—I tracked and found more bags of blood in the bathroom. Three in the sink, floating in warm water. Three on the counter. I snatched up a warmed bag, water dripping from it, tearing through the plastic, lapping up the blood so quickly that I didn't spill a drop.

I drained that first bag. Then the second and third.

It wasn't enough. It wasn't ever going to be enough.

I consumed the fourth bag, feeling it was cold but not caring.

Then the fifth.

I tried to slow down. I was behaving like a ... like a blood-starved vampire. A wounded, blood-starved vampire.

The sixth bag was gone, and there were no more ... I worked back through the IV bags, looking for lingering drops and attempting to squeeze them out.

The plastic disintegrated in my shaking hands.

It wasn't going to be enough.

I could hear heartbeats ... including two that were only steps away.

Magical blood was thrumming through their veins.

Human blood wasn't ever going to fill this gaping hole in my core. But magical blood...strong, potent powerful blood. If I could take down the necromancer, I knew instinctively that her blood would sustain me for months...a year, perhaps.

And if I drained her...would I gain an immunity to her magic?

I was at the door before I'd even decided to move. I was ready to break the lock, but realized that it wasn't actually engaged.

I laughed at their carelessness.

The sound of that laughter in my own ears was...creepy. Evil. Dark and soulless.

I didn't care.

Slowly, I turned the door's handle.

I would stalk them through the house. I would drain every last drop of them. I would eat the flesh of their hearts.

Then magic slammed against me. Necromancy.

Pain reverberated through my limbs. I stumbled, falling back to the thickly carpeted floor.

They had warded the door against me.

I wouldn't be murdering anyone else this day.

Thank God.

Oh, thank God.

I crawled away, putting the bed between me and the door, with the wall at my back. Light edged the curtains of the window above me. It was full day. I must have been out for hours.

I tucked my knees into my chest, closing my eyes and trying to feel for Kett. Trying to reach out to my master through our shared blood, our shared magic.

But I couldn't feel him at all.

I could still hear the heartbeats of everyone in the house. I didn't allow myself to count. Didn't allow myself to guess which heart belonged to which Adept.

I recalled the vision Rochelle had shared with me. I pictured myself, whole and happy, standing in the streets of London. I tried to remember every detail, to fall into the moment captured by the oracle's magic. The cobblestones had been damp, though it didn't appear to have been raining. They were a muddled shade of brown and red. I was standing by a deli of some sort. I could see rounds of gouda and a block of white cheddar in the window display.

God, I missed cheese. And bread. And food in general.

The endlessly beating hearts occupying the house broke through my resolve. The hunger spiked again. I tamped it down, curling into a fetal position on the floor.

If I just stayed still enough, it would pass. Eventually, I would fall into an undead state. But even if I did, I knew I would wake again. For London. The oracle had shown me that much.

That was assuming the future was set in stone, though.

Which I didn't actually believe.

I had foiled death, after all. And with a necromancer in the house, it was much easier to believe that without Kett to hold me in the world, the reaper would have her way.

Magic rippled through the bedroom, flitting across my eyelids. The door opened and someone stepped in.

Someone without a heartbeat.

He paused, closing the door behind him and engaging the lock.

Dear God ... they had sent someone to put me out of my misery.

Unfortunately for him, I wasn't ready to give up.

My eyes felt dry and sticky, but I forced them open, gathering my numb limbs underneath me. I crouched, keeping as low behind the bed as I could. My hands were splayed on the thick carpet, ready to spring up and over. Ready to fight whoever was standing silently just inside the door.

My fingers were shockingly thin. Almost skeletal. Clumps of my hair littered the floor around me. I was falling apart.

"Jasmine?"

It took me a moment to register his voice. I glanced toward the curtained window, noting that it was dark outside. Even more hours had passed.

Which made sense. Because Benjamin Garrick couldn't bear the sun.

They had sent a vampire to deal with another vampire. A wounded, decaying vampire. Unfortunately, while Benjamin might technically have been older than me in his new incarnation, he was nowhere near as strong.

Except I wasn't feeling particularly strong ...

"I'm stepping around the bed."

"No!" The word erupted from my throat, feeling like it had to shred my vocal cords in order to pass. The fear that had gotten me partially onto my feet drained away. I slumped backward, resting against the wall, half crouched.

"I brought blood," Benjamin said, unzipping something.

"It's not enough," I whispered. "It's not...potent enough."

He stepped farther into the room, just close enough to see me over the green-tufted silk duvet that topped the bed. He stilled, flicking his dark-brown eyes over me in concern. Then he attempted to school the shock out of his expression.

He took another step, resting his satchel on the bed. Then he pulled an IV bag filled with blood out of it. "This is mine, actually."

I laughed harshly. "Taunting me isn't a great idea, Benjamin."

"I'm making you an offer."

"What's that? Your blood?"

"Yes."

Dread shocked me to silence. Then the hunger rose up again...like a predator living within me...and it...looked at Benjamin. I squeezed my eyes shut. "Don't be ridiculous."

Benjamin punctured the bag of blood. The scent hit me, and a low, rolling growl leaked out between my clenched teeth. Then he started drinking.

I lunged.

One moment, I was trying to control myself. The next, I was inches away from Benjamin, fangs bared.

He didn't flinch. He did, however, blink. Then he took another sip of the blood. He was drinking it through a stainless steel straw.

I clenched my fingers into fists, hearing the bones crunch as I forced them to move. But I couldn't step back. I could keep myself suspended there, in check, but I couldn't step away.

Benjamin drained the IV bag. I watched him pull the liquid into his mouth and down his throat. The veins in his neck plumped.

"They sent you in here," I murmured, finally gaining control of my voice. "Like a sacrificial cow."

Benjamin laughed quietly. "Bull. Like a sacrificial bull."

He turned to the bed, carefully rolling up the spent IV bag, tucking it away, and pulling out another full of blood.

"I'm not drinking from you," I said, already knowing that I was lying. Knowing that if I didn't get him out of the room somehow, I would drain him dry. And unlike me, Benjamin would die. His own master had died in remaking him. The blood that animated him wasn't strong enough to feed me and sustain him at the same time.

The dark-haired vampire didn't reply. He stuck his straw into the fresh bag of blood, then turned back to me, slowly drinking from it.

I was standing way too close, but he didn't step back. His movements were slow but steady. I didn't scare him. Knowing Benjamin's history, I would have imagined that little did. Except Kett, the executioner.

But then, Kett scared me too.

"How many bags of blood did you bring?"

"Ten in the bag. One and a half gone now."

"I drank four before … and then … six more … and I'm … not …"

"I drank three before I came in," Benjamin said, ignoring my inability to express myself. "I drink about three a day, usually. I tried to drink less, because three seemed like too much. But Kett wants me to drink as much as I want."

"I'm not going to drink from you, Ben," I whispered. Then I licked my lips.

His gaze dropped to my mouth. Just for a blink, then he was looking into my eyes again.

A completely different kind of desire fluttered through my belly.

Oh God, no.

I hadn't felt any sensation even remotely sexual since my reawakening. At first, all my thought had been consumed by drinking Kett's blood and figuring out how much of me had survived the transition. Then I'd been focused on figuring out how to function, how to craft a new life for myself. But many vampires—if not most—equated the drinking of blood with sex.

Kett certainly did. And he hadn't drunk my blood since before he'd made me his child. That was a line he wasn't interested in crossing, no matter what he might have said to Wisteria when he'd promised to remake her. After I became a vampire, I hadn't had any desire to cross the line between feeding and sex either.

Until now. With Benjamin Garrick.

"Jasmine?" The dark-haired vampire touched my cheek, ghosting his fingers across my skin. I could sense how withered I felt beneath his fingertips. "The witches need you. And the oracle."

"So they sent you."

"You're stronger than me. You can walk in the day. The warriors have fallen. Except you."

"I can't…I can't drink from you Benjamin…it's wrong…morally."

"Morally? Because…of you and Kett?"

"No. No. We're not…we're not together like that."

"But he feeds you, yes? Feeds from you?"

"Yes. And no. I don't think he needs to drink very often. But he doesn't drink from me."

"Then what's so immoral about you drinking from me?"

"You and me, we're not...I shouldn't be stealing experiences from you. And...you can't drink from me. Things like this should be...reciprocal."

Benjamin was watching me too closely, listening carefully, dissecting my words. I remembered him in the Talbots' basement, holding his fountain pen, studiously bent over his notebook. I wondered how much of this encounter would go in the chronicle he was writing.

"You...for you, drinking blood from me is like sex?"

"I...I don't know. I've never done it before."

"You drink from Kett. You drank from him when he turned you."

I frowned. "Yes, but I don't really remember it. I was dying."

Benjamin nodded thoughtfully. He had drained the second bag of blood.

"What about you?" I asked. "Do you remember drinking from Nigel?"

"I do. He had to help. I couldn't break through his skin."

"From his neck?" I really shouldn't have been asking such intimate questions—because I couldn't take my gaze off Benjamin, off the blood moving through the veins of his own neck.

"Yes. Where else would I drink from?"

An inappropriate smile spread across my face as all the places Kett had drunk from me when I was human sprang to mind. All the places I could drink from Benjamin.

"You're too young!" I blurted. And finally, I managed to step back, diverting my gaze to the floor.

"Too young?" Benjamin echoed. "Too young to nourish you? Because you're worried about hurting me?"

"Yes." Answering with that half-truth, I stepped back around the bed, retreating from everything the predator wedged down deeply inside me was raging for … blood and sex … connection, dominion …

I sat down, pressing my back to the wall. And Benjamin followed me. He crouched down before me, a third bag of blood in his hands.

I really shouldn't have been counting.

He'd pushed up the sleeves of his thin sweater. A mass of scar tissue wreathed his left wrist.

Anger flashed through me. Suddenly I was holding his hand, though I was careful to not touch the wounded tissue. "What's this? Who did this to you?"

"You know, Jasmine. From the bracelet."

Right. Benjamin usually wore a necromancy working that helped him keep his vampire nature in check. I hadn't realized that it hurt him so badly.

I was still holding him. I should have let him go.

"It should heal. It should have healed already."

Benjamin shrugged. "If you won't drink from me, then maybe you want some of this?" He lifted the IV bag in his right hand, completely ignoring that I was still holding his left wrist.

He pierced the plastic bag with the straw before I answered. Then he sipped from it deeply.

I held him fast by the wrist, watching the muscles of his neck while he swallowed.

Then Benjamin offered me the blood, offered me the straw. And God help me, I leaned forward and took a sip.

He watched my mouth.

I took another sip.

His gaze flicked up to meet mine. The red of his magic was ringing his dark-brown eyes.

"I won't bite your neck," I said.

"Where, then?"

"Your wrist." I flicked my gaze to his left wrist. I still held his arm aloft between us.

"Okay."

"And…and we need a safe word."

A grin lit up Benjamin's face, transforming him from a serious and gentle person…into a sexy, available man. "Like what? Avocado?"

I laughed despite myself. "Avocado it is. If you feel light-headed…or…worried."

"I already feel light-headed." He was still smiling, still easy, still perfectly ready to let me feed on him. Like he was prey.

Except he wasn't prey. He was like me. A vampire. And the offer of his blood was a thing more profound than either of us had the experience to understand.

"At least tell me you're nineteen. Twenty?"

Benjamin chuckled. "I'm older than you."

"How do you figure that?"

"I was turned in October 2016. And you?"

"May 2017. But that doesn't count."

"That's exactly what counts. That's exactly how vampires measure the passage of time. And we're vampires, Jasmine." He took another sip through the stainless steel straw.

"We are." I sighed. "We are vampires."

Benjamin shifted forward, pressing his wrist into my hand. I eased my grip, allowing him to settle his scarred skin against my lips.

"Avocado," I whispered.

He nodded.

Keeping my gaze locked to his, I bit down. I found a vein by instinct, sealing my lips over the wound I'd created. His blood slowly seeped into my mouth. And I drank, sipping. I shuddered as the taste of him—sugary sweet and pleasantly warm—slipped down my throat. But I tried to be gentle. I tried to be careful.

I saw the moment that my venom hit Benjamin. His shoulders relaxed and his grin became lazy, blurring his usual laser-like focus.

Then I saw the moment when he realized why two vampires sharing blood was as intimate as sex.

The red of his magic flooded his eyes, wiping the grin from his face. He moved to drink from the IV bag and fumbled. Tearing his gaze away from mine, he shoved the straw into his mouth, draining the bag swiftly.

Somehow, I managed to pull back from drinking, carefully licking the bite wound on his wrist and watching as his flesh healed, smoothing some of the scar tissue with it.

I cleared my throat, forcing myself to check in with him before I drank again. "Are you okay, Benjamin?"

"Yes." He shifted closer to me, curling his hand around the back of my neck and pressing me forward, encouraging me to bite him again. Except not on his wrist this time.

And God help me, I dropped his hand, reaching for his shoulders and drawing him toward me. "You can't bite me, Ben," I whispered against his neck.

He buried his hands in my hair, pressing his lips to my ear. "I know."

"My blood might kill you ... or drive you crazy. Or at least Kett thinks so."

"I know, Jasmine. I know." He leaned back, pulling me with him to the floor until I lay across him, until my hair fell down all around us. He wound his leg around mine, pinning my thigh against him.

I bit his neck. Blood spurted, but I got every drop.

He gasped. A soft sound, full of pleasure.

I drank. Blood flowed easier from a neck bite than a wrist.

Benjamin shifted against me, rubbing against me. Then, realizing what he was doing, he angled his hips slightly away.

I paused, pressing my tongue against the bite wound on his neck to stop the blood flow.

He reached down, adjusting himself, shifting his erection. "Sorry … I, um … I didn't know it still worked."

"It works," I murmured, feeling a sharp spike of desire in response to him admitting his own. "It's just not … I think it takes focus. Blood still flows through us."

"That's what you were worried about? Why you were worried about our ages? About being inappropriate?"

"I didn't want to … take the experience from you."

Benjamin laughed softly. "I'm not a virgin, Jasmine. As a human, I slept with plenty of people … girls. Mostly at some camp for cancer survivors, or in the hospital. There's nothing like fighting death to make you want to have sex. Actually, its more about the act than feeling any desire."

"Okay … I shouldn't have assumed."

"And you?" He trailed his fingers down my throat, then along my collarbone. My skin under his fingertips felt smooth. His blood was already helping me to heal.

"And me what? Am I a virgin?"

He laughed quietly. "You said you and Kett aren't together like this. So am I your first?"

That idea, that thought, made me pause. "This life is full of firsts."

"Yes." Benjamin grinned. "Isn't it fantastic?"

I locked my gaze to his. He lifted his head, kissing me softly, then catching my bottom lip in his teeth. I darted my tongue into his mouth.

"No biting me, Benjamin."

He nodded solemnly. "I'm going to need another bag of blood."

I shifted off him, untangling our limbs.

He stood, grabbing his satchel from the bed, shifting it to the bedside table, and pulling out another bag of blood. Then he reached down and offered me his hand. I took it.

He pulled me to my feet. And standing pressed against me, running his free hand up and down my curves—ass, hip, waist, and breast—he drank. Then he drew me onto the bed, offering me his body and his blood.

And I took both.

Benjamin fell asleep just before dawn. After checking to make sure that the curtains fully covered the windows so he wasn't in danger of accidental immolation, I wandered into the bathroom naked, checking my rib cage for wounds. I found none—and felt more whole than I had for days. I made sure that Benjamin still had blood—two bags of the ten he'd started the evening with. Then I got dressed.

A quick glance at my phone informed me that what had felt like days of slowly dying had actually been less than twenty-four hours.

When I tried the door, the magic that had been securing it had faded. Either Teresa had forgotten to renew the spell that had held me at bay even at the height of my hunger, or she'd somehow known that I'd regained my senses.

But when I checked, I found that her heartbeat didn't number alongside the others I could sense around me. So she had left the house. Presumably, Benjamin wouldn't need his bracelet replaced until sunset.

Embarrassment flashed through me as I realized why Teresa had removed the bracelet in the first place. She had understood that her son needed to be able to access his vampire magic, his vampire nature, in order to feed me. But that didn't tell me whether removing the bracelet had been done at Benjamin's request.

I peeked into Pearl's room. I could clearly see a glimmer of the stasis field that covered the elder witch, who appeared to be sleeping along with the two other occupants of the room, Burgundy and Olive.

Perhaps my seeing magic was a side effect of drinking from the elf? I wondered if that ability would fade, and how quickly.

Hearing the remainder of the heartbeats clustered below me, I wandered down to the basement. In the map room, Rochelle was sitting in one corner, either sketching or working on older sketches. Beau was sprawled next to her, sleeping.

The oracle looked up at my approach, offering me a smile, then taking a sip of something hot from a travel mug. I could see steam but couldn't smell whether it was coffee or tea.

Scarlett was suspended in the middle of the room, held within a column of magic that ran from floor to ceiling. Other tendrils—magical echoes of Rochelle's ivy vines and barbed wire—crisscrossed the ceiling and connected to various places on the map. And if I looked at it sideways, I was pretty certain I could see a shimmer of magic also running all along the edge of the baseboards.

Scarlett's strawberry-blond hair floated around her. She also appeared to be sleeping.

"Is Scarlett okay?" I asked Rochelle.

"As far as I can tell."

That wasn't particularly comforting.

"The barrier is up," the oracle said with great satisfaction.

"The barrier?"

Rochelle nodded. "Scarlett connected all the grid points."

I glanced at the map. "You ... you're saying the entire city is magically warded?"

"Seems so." A wickedly satisfied grin spread across the oracle's face. "The elves have retreated." She pointed to the stadium, which was now glowing a bright yellow-green on the map. "We still can't breach their wards, but we can track them through the city. And ... they can't get out."

"You've ... you and the witches have trapped the elves in the city."

"And you. We all did it." Rochelle returned her attention to her sketchbook, as if it wasn't an absolutely horrible idea to be trapped anywhere with murderous, rampaging elves.

Beau rolled to his feet. One second he was asleep and the next he was eyeing me while gently plucking the now empty mug out of Rochelle's hand. "I'll get you a refill."

"Thank you." Rochelle brushed her fingers against the back of her husband's hand, then he stalked past me without another word. Apparently, he found my blood-lust, and subsequent meltdown, disconcerting.

That made two of us.

"This is why you sent Benjamin to me," I said, returning my attention to the conversation. "Because when the elves start making a fuss, it's going to be difficult to stop them from hurting…everyone."

"Actually, it was his idea. And obviously, he was right. You look much better. Tony has been taking point on tech, but I'm certain he'd like your help. Thankfully, the elves' wards seem to come with some sort of diversion side effect. So no one nonmagical appears to have noticed that BC Place has been overrun by them. Not yet, at least. The diversion effect is giving Peggy trouble, actually, so she and Gabby are looking after the bakery. Tony said there weren't any events scheduled at the stadium this week, but other things…like people coming from out of town …" She waved her free hand. "… are going to need to be handled, cancelled …"

"You want me to help with…managing the media and the human public?"

Rochelle frowned. "That's your area of expertise, isn't it? Tech stuff."

"I thought you wanted me to hunt the elves."

"We won't kill them if they don't try to kill us. But you're right, the stalemate won't last. Pearl is going to need Scarlett. And she appears to be fueling the barrier spell right now."

"What? Fueling? Holy hell."

"Mory is on her way back here. I insisted. She's been awake for over twenty-four hours."

Thrown by the segue, I paused to scan the map, attempting to wrap my head around everything that had happened and what the hell we were going to do about it. Pearl was dying. Scarlett wasn't going to be much better off if this went on for more than a few days. She was a powerful witch, but personal magic wasn't an endless well. She'd burn out.

I heard a car pull into the driveway. And just a few moments later, Mory practically tumbled into the room, holding a dead turtle in one hand and a folded sheaf of paper in the other. Liam leaned into the doorway, scanning all the magic the room held with a look of distaste.

Beau slipped through the doorway silently, crossing to take up sentry by his pregnant wife and managing to keep an eye on all of us at once while carefully placing a steaming mug of whatever the oracle was drinking in her hands.

"She's there…Jade!" Mory said, speaking so quickly she was practically skipping words. "It took Ed hours to navigate the weird empty hallways toward the center. And I had some trouble maintaining my connection through the wards when he got too far away."

"Wait," I said. "Hallways? Like, inside the stadium itself?"

Liam nodded. "As far as we can see, they're in the process of building interior spaces for some reason, plus some sort of maze."

Mory ignored my interruption. "The elves have…they've got something magical on Jade. On her forehead. When Ed tries to look at it closely, it glows too brightly for me to see it, exactly. Then the camera shorts out."

"It's one of the gemstones." Every gaze in the room turned to me. I cleared my throat. "I didn't get a good look before Kett sent me to Pearl. But yeah, something bloody and bleeding in Jade's forehead, and the skinny, creepy elf…controlling her."

"She's not controlling her all that well." Mory smirked, full of satisfaction, as she tapped the sheaf of papers on top of the turtle's hard shell. "The elf, that elf, is trying to make Jade fix some sort of magical device. I think that's what's shorting out the camera. I don't actually get any audio through Ed, like maybe he doesn't pick up vibrations the same way I do." She turned her gaze on Rochelle. "When you texted, Liam wanted to continue mapping. But I wanted you to know firsthand. Jade's alive."

The sorcerer crossed his arms belligerently. "You've barely covered a third of the footprint."

"You know I can't get Ed up the stairs," Mory snapped over her shoulder.

The dark-haired sorcerer sighed. "I meant barely a third of the main floor. You could have texted this information."

"I need breakfast. And a nap."

"Fine."

"So what do you think the elves are up to?" Beau asked, speaking for the first time since I'd entered the room. "Did you get any sense of... any plans? They waited two days to come for Rochelle, when coming the night they showed up at the club would have been a smarter tactical move."

Liam shook his head. Then he paused, thinking. "They're hurt. Or they were. Badly. In the first battle with Jade. They could barely walk when I saw them retreat into the stadium, carrying the others. And, like Mory said, they're having trouble controlling Jade. That's got to be draining resources." He glanced at the map, eyeing the glowing stadium. "We might actually have a window of opportunity to help them."

"And what about the dragons?" Beau asked, throwing the question out to all of us. "Drake was supposed to go to Jade's father."

"But Drake also said that the warrior... and the healer had been called away." Mory looked at me for confirmation. "After the elves showed up at the dance club."

I nodded. I'd heard Drake tell Jade that as well. "The guardian of North America is down. Jade's been taken. And if the guardians haven't responded, there's a reason. Let's hope that reason isn't that the rest of the world is going to hell at the same time. I died nine months ago, and I'm not a fan of doing so again any time soon."

Mory snorted a laugh.

I grinned at her. Trust a necromancer to like un-dead humor.

"So it's up to us then." Mory turned her intense and eager gaze on Rochelle, then me. "There must be something we can do to help Jade!"

Rochelle nodded. Then she flipped through to a specific page in her sketchbook and ripped it out. "I still haven't been able to see Jade. But I think maybe once Ed slipped through the elves' wards, I started to pick up more hints of what's to come."

A small person appeared by the oracle's shoulder. A brownie, wearing a black dress that ballooned out around her knees. She was wringing her large hands, glancing warily at each of us in turn. "I still can't get through, mistress." Her voice was gravelly.

Rochelle passed the sketch she'd ripped out of her book to the brownie, who took the paper reverently, peering at whatever was depicted on it.

"You understand, Blossom?" Rochelle asked. "A time will come and you will deliver that."

The brownie nodded. Then she disappeared.

"And us?" I asked Rochelle. "We just wait here for this … something to happen?"

"We've done what we can. So now we plan."

"Plan? Plan what? Storming the castle?"

Rochelle turned her white-eyed gaze to the wall where BC Place was still glowing bright green. "Yes."

"Yes?" I echoed incredulously. "I was being sarcastic. We can't take the elves down. You just said that we can't even get through their wards!"

"Except Ed," Mory interjected mildly.

"Great...a dead turtle piloted by a necromancer. Why aren't we already laying siege?" I glanced at them all in turn. They were all far too calm, too collected.

"We need more witches—"

"No," Scarlett said.

I flinched. I hadn't realized that she was aware enough to track our conversation, let alone participate in it.

"The future is at a balance point," the strawberry-blond witch murmured dreamily. "The oracle will tip it in the right direction."

I looked at Rochelle in disbelief.

She smiled softly, serenely. Her eyes were glowing white, her hands caked with black charcoal. Magic shifted around us, stirring through the map sketched on the walls...power etched in black and white. I could feel a low thrum underneath my feet...I could see a soft glow crisscrossing over the ceiling.

And...I believed.

I had to believe.

Just like I'd had to believe I would survive my childhood...my human death...the last twelve hours.

This was why the Godfrey coven had tied Rochelle to the witches' grid. And with all of us behind her, with all of our trust...the magic would follow.

"What comes next, oh oracle?" I whispered.

Rochelle bowed her head over her sketchbook, flipping to a blank page.

"Now we need Jade."

Acknowledgements

With thanks to:

My story & line editor
Scott Fitzgerald Gray

My proofreader
Pauline Nolet

My beta readers
Didi Brady, Cindy Cor, Terry Daigle, Angela
Flannery, Gael Fleming, Heather Lewis, Megan
Gayeski Pirajno, Beth Peters, and Diane
Sommers, Amy Smith, and Elise Wilson.

**For their continual encouragement,
feedback, & general advice**
SFWA
The Office
The Retreat

About the Author

Meghan Ciana Doidge is an award-winning writer based out of Salt Spring Island, British Columbia, Canada. She has a penchant for bloody love stories, superheroes, and the supernatural. She also has a thing for chocolate, potatoes, and cashmere yarn.

For recipes, giveaways, news, and glimpses of upcoming stories, please connect with Meghan on her:

New release mailing list, http://eepurl.com/AfFzz
Personal blog, www.madebymeghan.ca
Twitter, @mcdoidge
Facebook, Meghan Ciana Doidge
Email, info@madebymeghan.ca

Also by Meghan Ciana Doidge

Novels
After The Virus
Spirit Binder
Time Walker
Cupcakes, Trinkets, and Other Deadly Magic (Dowser 1)
Trinkets, Treasures, and Other Bloody Magic (Dowser 2)
Treasures, Demons, and Other Black Magic (Dowser 3)
I See Me (Oracle 1)
Shadows, Maps, and Other Ancient Magic (Dowser 4)
Maps, Artifacts, and Other Arcane Magic (Dowser 5)
I See You (Oracle 2)
Artifacts, Dragons, and Other Lethal Magic (Dowser 6)
I See Us (Oracle 3)
Catching Echoes (Reconstructionist 1)
Tangled Echoes (Reconstructionist 2)
Unleashing Echoes (Reconstructionist 3)
Champagne, Misfits, and Other Shady Magic (Dowser 7)
Misfits, Gemstones, and Other Shattered Magic (Dowser 8)

Novellas/Shorts
Love Lies Bleeding
The Graveyard Kiss (Reconstructionist 0.5)
Dawn Bytes (Reconstructionist 1.5)
An Uncut Key (Reconstructionist 2.5)
Graveyards, Visions, and Other Things that Byte (Dowser 8.5)

Please also consider leaving an honest
review at your point of sale outlet.

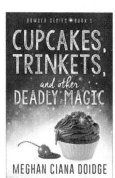

DOWSER SERIES ● Book 1

CUPCAKES, TRINKETS,
and other
DEADLY MAGIC

MEGHAN CIANA DOIDGE

DOWSER SERIES ● Book 2

TRINKETS, TREASURES,
and other
BLOODY MAGIC

MEGHAN CIANA DOIDGE

DOWSER SERIES ● Book 3

TREASURES, DEMONS,
and other
BLACK MAGIC

MEGHAN CIANA DOIDGE

DOWSER SERIES ● Book 4

SHADOWS, MAPS,
and other
ANCIENT MAGIC

MEGHAN CIANA DOIDGE

DOWSER SERIES ● Book 5

MAPS, ARTIFACTS,
and other
ARCANE MAGIC

MEGHAN CIANA DOIDGE

DOWSER SERIES ● Book 6

ARTIFACTS, DRAGONS,
and other
LETHAL MAGIC

MEGHAN CIANA DOIDGE

ORACLE SERIES ● Book 1

I SEE ME

MEGHAN CIANA DOIDGE

ORACLE SERIES ● Book 2

I SEE YOU

MEGHAN CIANA DOIDGE

ORACLE SERIES ● Book 3

I SEE US

MEGHAN CIANA DOIDGE

RECONSTRUCTIONIST SERIES ● Book 1

Catching Echoes

MEGHAN CIANA DOIDGE

RECONSTRUCTIONIST SERIES ● Book 2

Tangled Echoes

MEGHAN CIANA DOIDGE

RECONSTRUCTIONIST SERIES ● Book 3

Unleashing Echoes

MEGHAN CIANA DOIDGE

Made in the USA
Coppell, TX
05 August 2020

32463031R00127